TROUBLE ON THE WAY!

A lone horse, blood smeared on the saddle, wandered nervously into camp. Slipping from the darkness, Maddie spoke softly to the horse. It started to shy away, but the comfort of the fire and the instinctive sense of a beast for the gentleness of her words caused it to pause. Hands rubbing its mane, the horse nickered.

"What is it, fella? Where's the man who rode you?"

The blood was still wet. Somewhere out there, likely close, was a man wounded or worse. She spoke quietly to herself.

"Maddie, you left the frying pan and now you're going to jump right into the fire."

BOOKS BY MARK HERBKERSMAN

A WILD AND LONELY LAND

Collected Western Stories

By

Mark Herbkersman

Susan & Jeff –
Your friendship to us
has provided so many blessings
to us through the years. It means
many things to us, but most of all
it means love. We love you too,

Mark

DEDICATION

This book is respectfully dedicated to David Burris. One of the most successful – in all ways – men I have ever met. A devoted husband, father and friend, he knows the value of a job done right and done well. I wish you could all know him. He is one of the greatest gifts I have ever received.

ACKNOWLEDGEMENTS

This book writing gig is an emotion-filled journey. There are ups and downs and a few hairpin curves along the way. Each book is a journey of many months, but I'm not riding alone.

Joan Murphy has been helping me longer than anybody else. She reads, challenges and sometimes just gives me a look that says a lot! She is patient. I trust her.

Kay Phelps has been around for quite a spell. She tends to see word issues and loves to research and fill in the gaps. No detail is too small.

Readers of books are unaware of the writing, the reading, re-writing and re-reading, the correcting of awkward phrases and catching mistakes. This book has been read numerous times by Kay and Joni.

My wife, Marilyn, continues to put up with the whole book and writing thing. We have walked side by side for over three decades. I love you.

Joy, my daughter, once again worked to create a cover. This will be the third time she has blessed me with her talents.

My sincere thanks to my rapidly growing number of fans. Your encouragement makes a difference. When I hear you say, "I couldn't put it down!" it makes my heart glad.

And, most of all, to God. He gives me strength when I am weak, peace when I worry and a hope for the future.

Thank you all for blessing me in so many ways.

MESSAGE FROM THE AUTHOR

People ask me how I come up with characters in my books. Many of them come from seeing people in real life who are unique in some way. Then I create a character, usually – but not always - exaggerated from reality. Many times, inspiration comes from sitting and watching people go by. It might be the lines in their faces or a big bushy beard or something else that stands out. Characters are everywhere. My imagination does the rest.

Short stories help me to flesh out characters who may appear in full length novels later. This collection includes new characters who may appear in later stories, God willing. The more I write, the more ideas clutter my mind, especially with the Henry family and their friends. They are, indeed, a magnificent family.

I have wanted to write a book about a lady gunslinger. It poses a bit of an issue in many ways, to make a woman tough but still be a woman in the traditional sense. There are two of them in this book – Josie and Maddie. And, of course, they belong to the illustrious Henry family.

Let me know what you think.

See **Mark Herbkersman Author** on Facebook.

Contents

A WILD AND LONELY LAND

Pacheco dropped his package and leapt into the path of the running horses, his arms upraised. He crossed himself and spoke a command to the horses.

"Whoa!"

Moments before, standing at the edge of the boardwalk with his meager purchases in a package under his arm, Pacheco took a few moments to watch the local children playing in the street. He found himself transported to his own boyhood in Juarez. They were days of play, exploration, his mother's tortillas and his father's easy laughter. He smiled as a game of leapfrog erupted into playful scrambling and giggles.

A sound came to his ear, and something in his mind sharpened and shifted. He turned to see a buckboard, running full out, the bay horses matched, magnificent and muscled. They were headed into a turn, skidding sideways and suddenly straight for the children.

It was a gift of God, some said, the way animals of all kinds responded to Pacheco. It had always been this way and it was the same now. The horses of Creed Taylor skidded to a halt, throwing Creed to his knees and over the footboard to the singletrees. He wavered, groping at the air until he landed in the dust at the heels of one horse.

His fine, store bought suit was covered with the dust of the street and his hat was crushed. Crawling out, he fumed, aware that bystanders had witnessed this humiliation. Standing and dusting off his trousers, he strode with burning anger to where Pacheco stood, proceeding to backhand the Mexican.

Though his immediate instinct was to run a blade through this man's gut, Pacheco knew to do so would result in a quick hemp noose. He let this man vent and walk away with his false dignity. Still, Pacheco's hand moved to his back, where the razor-sharp blade was sheathed crossways along his belt.

Children in the street and bystanders on the walks stood transfixed and silent. Though despising Creed Taylor, they held a respectful fear.

"Taylor! Come on now! You got no cause to hurt that man."

Sheriff Burr Evans was one of the few who spoke their minds to Taylor. It was not a friendship, for no one was a friend with Taylor. It was a mutual grudging regard between men who fought in the War Between the States. Evans was not intimidated by Taylor's bluff and bluster. And Taylor listened – sometimes – to Burr Evans. Still, neither gave the other the respect of a first name.

"Crazy Mexican stopped my team, Evans! Look at my suit!"

"From the looks of it, you were gonna hurt them young'uns, Taylor. Haven't I told you about running the team in town?" He looked to Pacheco. "Better get out of here. You passin' through?"

"Looking for some friends near here. Name of Martinez."

Evans glanced over at Taylor and then back.

"Their place is over east. 'Bout two hours ride. Aim at the twin peaks and then go north."

"Thank you, Sheriff."

Taylor was ruffled. "Martinez won't be there long. Best you hurry him up. I suggested he move somewhere south – far south. He's got no right to that valley – it should belong to those who came first. Not some second-hand immigrants."

Pacheco could not resist. "You mean, señor, it should belong to the Indians? They were here first."

Taylor reddened. Evans couldn't help but grin. He looked to Pacheco. "I suggest you move along."

✿ ✿ ✿ ✿ ✿

Pacheco was a wandering man, preferring to keep to himself. He'd been everywhere but never anywhere very important. Ever since that day he crossed the Rio Grande, he'd never once returned to see his family.

Coming into the little town of Las Cruces those long years ago, Pacheco was crossing the street and looked up as a gringo nearly ran him down on a horse that looked massive from that angle. The man was already red faced over something and cussed at him. Pacheco remembered hearing the words as he quickly got out of the way.

"Get the Mex! I'll teach him to watch more closely."

Pacheco knew to get lost. Slipping between buildings

where a horse couldn't fit, he hid from pursuit by heading north. Somehow, for all these decades, Pacheco rarely turned south. Accustomed to the desert, the growing purple of the mountains drew him onward and it was the mountains that kept him.

The years had not all been good. Far from it, really. Living as a small man amidst the towering mountains and men of the West had changed him. Never settled, he wandered, an odd figure due to his stature. Not against skirting the edge of the law, he never ventured far over the line. Yet, when there was a need for help, Pacheco did what was needed. Though small, Pacheco was dangerous. Advanced in age, he was still fast. Despite narrow blades, his knives were sharp.

Friends were many and spread throughout the West. Along the trails and in the Mexican communities, the name of Pacheco had respect.

It was interesting the way word was passed in the vast distances of the West. There was, of course, mail that could be sent to a last known location. It was unreliable and letters often languished for years, forgotten in a stack in some remote town. The recipient could be dead or had no reason to expect anything. More often than not, word was passed by mouth and it was surprising how many times the message found its way to the intended recipient, many hundreds or even thousands of miles away.

A month ago, he was in a small town buying a few items for his saddlebags, and a Mexican swamper approached him.

"I have a message for Pacheco if you know him."

"I do. I will pass the message on. What is it?"

"Pacheco is needed." Questioned further, the man gave a name and place. Pacheco left the next morning. He didn't ride with haste, as the message was old enough that any urgency was long past. But he rode with purpose through a wild and lonely land.

Now he topped a small rise and saw the Martinez ranch. It was not a large place, but a place of those who worked hard and made do with what they had. Most ranchers started just this way and tightened their belts during the early lean years. Pacheco had known many ranchers over his years and travels, and thought of how many forgot what it was like when they started. Years of struggle and drought and living without tended to precede better years - if those better years ever arrived. So much could happen in the building of a dream. More than one successful rancher built large herds, erected a frame house, sighed with contentment at a healthy bank balance, then died, thrown from a running horse plunging a hoof into a prairie dog hole.

The Martinez ranch was a struggling ranch. Built of the products of the land, the buildings were rough-hewn log and made for weathering storms. Still, there was a fine arrangement of the few buildings and Pacheco smiled at the flowers growing by the front steps. The placement showed taste in view.

A dog ran from the barn and barked as he approached. A small woman in her middle years came from the doorway of the cabin, shading her eyes from the sun. Within the door, Pacheco could see what appeared to be a Sharps rifle leaning easy to hand.

"Muy Buenos, Valencia."

The woman walked a few feet further, squinting. Suddenly she smiled with delight.

"Pacheco!" Turning to the barn and the side of the house, she shouted. "It is safe! All is well. It is Pacheco!"

From the side of the house came a young man carrying a rifle, who Pacheco took to be in his early teens. Then, turning to the barn he saw a young lady emerge from the shadows. The pistol she held had seen use. Pacheco could not miss her beauty or the kindness in her eyes. He turned back to the woman before him.

"Valencia, it is good to see you." He looked around. "Where is Carlos?"

"He is inside, Pacheco. He was shot two months ago. Very bad. For many days we thought for sure he would die. Even after all these weeks, he has bad days when I fear he fails again. I do not know."

Pacheco nodded and looked at Valencia. There was a time in his younger years when she had been in his heart – and his arms - but his need to wander forced her to choose and she chose Carlos. He admitted it was a good choice, and a couple times over the years their paths had crossed. But the last time was several years back. She and Carlos were devoted to each other.

"The years have been good to you, Valencia."

She smiled. "Thank you, Pacheco. You lie very well. We all change with the years. Beauty is replaced by wisdom. In my case, it has been replaced by many wrinkles!" She laughed and then her eyes turned grave. "I knew you'd come if you received word." Gesturing to the young man, she said, "This is Alberto, my son. When Carlos found I was with child he strutted around like a champion rooster!" Then she turned to the young woman. "This is Amalita, the daughter of my sister. Her mother passed five years ago and Amalita came to live with us. Her beauty is noticed and men's gazes are not all with honorable intent. Still, she is wise and she will choose her man someday."

"You have a nice ranch here."

"We came here seven years ago. We filed on the land legally, but there are those who want it. There is an opening to an inner valley that is lush and with plentiful water. Señor Taylor has offered to buy and when we refused he has sought to take it."

"Is it he that shot Carlos? I met a gringo in town by that name. A most unpleasant man."

"No, but it was one of his men. A man named Gil Linder. Carlos went to check on some of the cattle and found Linder looking over the area. Linder claimed Carlos pulled a gun on him. You and I know Carlos would never do such a thing. But, of course, we are Mexicans. Sheriff Evans wanted to do something, but he has no power out of town. One of Taylor's other hands was a good man and found Carlos and brought him in, then kept riding. Creed Taylor wants the land, but I do not think – yet – that he will resort to murder. I think Linder acted on his own. The truth remains that Linder still rides for Taylor. But Pacheco! Please, come inside. Alberto will see to your horse."

Carlos was sitting in a curtained off sleeping area, looking very haggard and pale. Weariness shown in his eyes, but there was also determination. Pacheco looked deep and saw that Carlos might never be the same, but he would live. Already a very small man, he was wasted with his body's fight. Looking at Pacheco, he smiled. His voice was faint.

"Pacheco!"

"Carlos! What are you doing in bed? You are lazy!"

"Yes, my friend." A shallow laugh erupted. "My wife – who I won from you – is a hard worker so I need not trouble myself with chores. I just eat and sleep!"

Both men chuckled. Carlos coughed.

"You have built a fine home, Carlos. But I hear you have had problems."

"Yes. It is what happens when you find a treasure and someone decides they want it." He looked out the window. "Pacheco, this place is a dream waiting to happen. The valley is my family's future. I may not live to see what this place becomes, but I see it in my mind. Alberto will have a place to stand proud. He is a fine boy, my friend."

"He is a fine boy, Carlos. And this place is beautiful."

"And it is a good feeling – to know one is building for a reason. Yes, I have been healing slowly, but that is to be expected. I was so close to death I actually saw my Savior walking to me. I reached towards Him, but then it seemed like He said I was to stay a while longer. Then a rider found me and brought me home. But I no longer fear death, Pacheco. For I saw – I saw! But I must get well and continue."

He coughed again and leaned back.

"Rest now, Carlos."

❧❧ ❧❧ ❧❧ ❧❧ ❧❧

Three days later, Pacheco rode into town to speak to the sheriff. He tied his horse behind the livery. Slipping between the store and the jail, he stepped to the boardwalk and entered the sheriff's office.

Burr Evans sat looking at circulars of wanted men and drinking a cup of coffee. He looked up and his eyes widened.

"I know you're not here to just say hello. Might's well have a seat."

"Not many would want me to sit, señor."

"Well, I ain't made that way." He gestured to the stove. "Coffee's hot."

Pacheco filled a cup and sat. The sheriff scratched his chin.

"I didn't get your name."

"I am called Pacheco."

"Would you have knifed Taylor if he did more the other day?"

"It crossed my mind, Sheriff. But I would not have killed him." He smiled.

"I knew by the way your hand went back. Besides, I hear things. Pacheco. Not a common name, but a name with meaning behind it. On the back trails it's a name that holds respect. Heard it connected to a friend of mine a few years ago."

"Who might that be?"

"Liam Henry."

"He is a good man to share the trail."

Evans nodded. Then, as if something was settled in his mind, he changed the subject. "You friends with Martinez?"

Pacheco smiled. "In a way. His wife would be my wife if I could have given up looking over the next hill."

"Well, I heard about the shooting. Unfortunately, I have no authority outside of town. But it doesn't keep me from picking up bits and pieces, which is why you're here – am I right?"

"I am not afraid of Taylor, Sheriff, and these are my friends. Carlos sent for me. I want you to know that I will observe the law – as best I can. But I will defend myself and my friends. What can you tell me about Taylor?"

"Taylor's a tough man and can be ruthless. There is also something inside that respects a fighting man. I can't help thinking that a few years down the line he and Martinez could actually dine together."

"It is always possible, Sheriff, but changing minds and hearts takes a bit of time. There is always the suspicion and the feeling of threat to a lifestyle or a way of belief. Besides, there is this man – Linder."

"A vicious man. Will shoot at the drop of a hat. He's caused a bit of a ruckus now and then, but Taylor has given strict instructions to keep the town peaceful. He is big on appearances. Since Carlos was shot, Taylor has drifted a few cattle over on Martinez range. He thinks Carlos is out of the game and that, eventually, the ranch will be abandoned." The sheriff paused. "But sometimes I have too much time on my hands, so I sit and observe and I see things that make me wonder. There's an angle that I think

Creed Taylor is missing altogether."

"What is that?"

"More than once I been out riding over the hills to the old mines. There used to be silver mines a few miles out till the veins played out. Now they're just holes. Makes for a nice ride. I think of them when they were bustling with people and the money seemed to flow." He looked squarely at Pacheco. "Lonely place, really. Only there's more traffic than you might think out there. Two people keep showing up. The same two people."

"Who are they?"

"Amalita…and Jason Taylor."

Pacheco's eyes widened. "Jason is Creed Taylor's son?"

"Yes. And he is – unlike his father – a fine young man."

Pacheco nodded and smiled. "If only we could be as innocent as young love, señor."

Evans smiled. "Ain't that the truth?"

"Is there more to the feud between Taylor and Carlos than land? I sense there is a deep dislike for my friend."

"Yes, there is. Of course, Taylor needs to be better than others. Got most of this town wary of him and the rest eating out of his hand somewhere. Carlos being a Mex feeds into that. The trouble deepened shortly after Martinez filed on his land, when we had a Founders Day shindig. Sewing and baking and such. Valencia took a ribbon in pie making." He smiled and patted his stomach. "I was a judge. That was an enjoyable day. Both Taylor and Martinez entered the sharpshooting contest. Taylor is an excellent shot. He puffed up and bragged it around that he would win easily. Contest time came and he seen Martinez walk up. Martinez nodded to him and the others, and Taylor made a crack about Martinez being as small as a boy and just laughed – until Martinez outshot him and took the ribbon. Taylor's had it out for him ever since."

"The plot thickens."

"It most certainly does. Taylor lost face. And I learned something about Carlos Martinez that day. As he was leaving town, he passed Widow Grant's place. Youngsters had taken down some of the rails of her fence and she was struggling to get it fixed. Carlos stopped his wagon and the family got down and helped her put the fence back together. Valencia came back a week later and brought the widow a pie. That is something we need more of around here."

"Sheriff, my being Mexican does not seem to bother you."

"I was raised on the border. My father had vaqueros. They were part of our family until my father was killed and we all moved on."

"Who killed him, señor?"

Sheriff Evans raised his eyebrows.

"A gringo." He stood and offered his hand to Pacheco

"Gracias, Sheriff Evans."

Watching Pacheco slip behind the buildings, Burr Evans scratched his jaw and, hitching his gun belt, went out to check the town.

✿ ✿ ✿ ✿ ✿

Pacheco and Alberto spent a couple weeks driving Taylor's cattle off Martinez range. It did not seem that Taylor worried much as his cattle seemed to roam freely. Perhaps it was appearance that mattered for Taylor. If there was anything said of his cattle, he could always claim they wandered of their own choice. If they just slowly encroached it would just be understood it was his range by possession. When Martinez moved out he would then quietly file.

Alberto was smart and Pacheco taught him the ways of the range, such as riding up a hill to the point where he could see over and not skyline himself. Sometimes they would stop and make coffee and Alberto was amazed at Pacheco's ability to make a fire with so little smoke. Some of the lessons were those of a wilder range, but they were valuable nonetheless. This range was still on the ragged edge of the wild.

One day he saw dust in the distance. Alberto was on the other side of the valley. Pacheco stared off and observed the dust as it moved. A horse and rider, coming from the direction of the ranch and headed towards the old mines.

Another rendezvous of love? That night he went to the barn. Amalita's saddle blanket was damp.

❦ ❦ ❦ ❦ ❦

Carlos continued to improve, and finally walked outdoors to the corral. He made this a daily habit. Valencia walked with him at first, but then let him be as he improved.

A couple weeks went by and he stood with Valencia in the afternoon sun watching the horses. How he longed to ride again. He was just contemplating trying to get on when he heard hoof beats approaching. Turning, he saw Creed Taylor, Linder and a couple others ride into the ranch yard. Taylor pulled up and looked around.

"Came to see if you'd moved on yet, Martinez. Still hanging on? Looks like you can't pull your weight."

"I have no intention of leaving, Taylor. I filed fair and this land is mine."

Linder leaned on his saddle horn. "Maybe I shoulda shot twice. Might be the second shot will happen right now."

"Señor Taylor? Is this your order – for Linder to shoot?"

Taylor reddened.

"We don't need shooting. You'll leave soon enough."

Linder smirked.

"Boss? A little lead would seal the ranch deal."

A voice came from beside the barn to their left.

"Even touch that gun and I'll blow you out of the saddle."

Linder stopped cold. Turning his head, he saw Pacheco at the corner of the barn, the large black bore of a Sharps leveled at him.

"Maybe I need to fire two shots, Mex."

"You'll have to gamble that I miss with my first shot, Linder. That is not likely."

"Life is always a gamble, Mex."

Taylor jumped in. "Shut up, Linder. Keep loose and don't go near your gun!"

Another voice spoke to the right. It was Burr Evans.

"Wise idea."

Taylor spoke. "You're out of your jurisdiction, Evans."

"I may not be sheriff out here, but I'm still a law abiding citizen. And what is happening here is wrong and you know it, Creed. Call off your dog. Any firing starts and you'll be in the middle of it."

"I tell you again, Martinez. Leave." He looked to the Sheriff. "Election coming, Evans."

‹♦› ‹♦› ‹♦› ‹♦› ‹♦›

A few days later, riding alone, Pacheco approached the old mines and saw dust in the distance. Squinting, he then turned and saw another dust cloud.

Amalita meeting Jason Taylor again.

Drawn by movement, he glanced further and saw a third dust cloud.

Who could this be?

Waiting until the first two dust clouds met and settled, he brought his horse to a canter. Slowing as he approached a hillside of mine tailings, he walked the horse around and glimpsed Amalita and Jason Taylor in an embrace. A hoof clipping a rock broke them apart suddenly and they looked around. Jason dropped his hand to his belt.

"No need to be alarmed, Señor Jason. My problems are with your father, not you." He smiled. "Besides, young love is what the future is made of."

Amalita brushed her hair away from her face.

"Why are you here, Pacheco?"

"I knew you two were seeing each other and decided it

was the best way to talk to young Taylor here." He slouched in the saddle. "Are your intentions towards Amalita honorable, Señor Taylor?"

"I love her, sir. We wish to be married, but my father would not approve."

"That is true, señor. I suspect it will get worse before there is a chance for it to get better. Your father is harsh and set on his plans."

"He is."

"Did you know you were followed, Señor Taylor?"

"Followed?"

"They say 'love is blind.' And so it is. Someone followed you."

Suddenly a terrified scream turned their heads.

"Evie!" Jason turned and ran towards the sound, Amalita close behind. Pacheco dropped from his horse and followed.

ৎ৲ ৎ৲ ৎ৲ ৎ৲ ৎ৲

Rounding the hillside, they spotted a horse standing in the tall grass. Another muffled scream erupted and they ran forward, finding a hole in the ground. Jason Taylor dropped to his knees and looked down the hole.

"Evie!"

He heard sobbing, then a cry. "Jason! Help me!"

It was a small hole, apparently an old air shaft. The sides crumbled and trickled dirt downward. Pacheco gave a warning: "The shaft is old. It would not take much to collapse a side. Amalita, you and I need to back away. Jason, you move as little as possible. Try to calm her down."

"Evie! I'm here. What happened?"

More sobs. It was clear the girl was at least fifteen or twenty feet down and the shaft was very narrow. Little trickles of soil could be heard falling within. It would not take much for the shaft to collapse and bury Evie.

"I was following you. I wanted to see Amalita. I stepped off my horse and fell into this hole. My leg hurts real bad. It's all twisted. I'm stuck. Please help me, Jason!"

Pacheco's brow furrowed.

"How old is she, Jason?"

"Nine. She's small. None of us can fit down the shaft." He shouted down the hole. "Evie, move as little as possible. We need help to get you out."

Amalita spoke.

"Carlos!"

Jason and Pacheco looked to her.

"Carlos can fit. He is small anyway. Since he was shot he has lost much weight. He could go down."

Pacheco nodded.

"Ride, Amalita! Ride like the wind! Time is important."

Moments later they heard the sound of running hoof beats fading into the distance.

⚜ ⚜ ⚜ ⚜ ⚜

"Boss, want me to get the men and sneak up on the house? Pacheco rode off a while back."

"No, Linder. Let's get a bunch more of our beef deep

into their range."

Several men rode with them as they pushed the cattle. Spread across the valley, they had several hundred head moving. Creed Taylor and Linder sat atop a rise, watching.

"Think this'll work, Boss?"

"Cattle give ownership, Linder. The more of our cattle there are, the smaller Martinez looks."

Linder suddenly rose in his stirrups and squinted into the distance. He pointed and Creed Taylor turned to look.

"Running horse." Linder sat. "Looks like a woman!"

Taylor stared a few moments. "It's that girl that lives with Martinez."

As they looked, they saw the horse turn. Amalita had spotted the riders and, a few minutes later, her horse lathered, she pulled up before Creed Taylor.

"You shouldn't be on Martinez range, Taylor! But it doesn't matter right now. Evie has fallen into an old air shaft at the mines. The only one small enough to get her would be Carlos. I'm riding for the ranch!"

Creed Taylor suddenly looked alarmed.

"What was she doing there?"

"No time for that now. I must ride hard. But my horse needs a few minutes to rest."

"Linder! Give her your horse!"

"My horse?"

"She needs to move fast! Her horse is spent. Give her your horse!"

With that, Amalita switched horses and rode. Creed Taylor spurred his horse to the mines.

❧❦ ❧❦ ❧❦ ❧❦ ❧❦

Jason and Pacheco heard running horses. Pacheco motioned Jason to stay and ran around the hill as Creed Taylor and five men rode up the trail.

"Whoa!" The horses and men reined in hard.

"We saw Amalita. Where's my daughter?"

"Leave the horses here, señor, and do not run or disturb the ground. Jason is at the hole just ahead. We don't want it to cave in."

Creed Taylor strode around the bend and, seeing Jason at the hole, stopped. His voice was plaintive as he spoke softly.

"Can you tell if she's hurt, Jason?"

"Says her leg is hurt and twisted, Pa." Jason looked down the hole. "Pa's here, Evie!"

Creed Taylor could hear a vague sobbing voice. "Pa." Taylor looked to Pacheco.

"She is small, señor, and has fallen a long ways. The hole also is small and not too solid. Amalita had the idea that Carlos would fit down the hole. He has lost a lot of weight since your man Linder shot him. Maybe that will actually turn out good."

Taylor looked around.

"What were you all doing here, Jason? And why was Evie here?"

"Pa, now's not the time to discuss this, but I was riding to see Amalita. Evie followed and fell into the hole."

"You and that Mex girl? You been riding off with her?"

"Yes, Pa! I love her."

"I forbid it!"

"Not your choice anymore, Pa. You can have your ways, but I'm not going to be like that."

"How dare…"

A scream came from Evie.

"I'm slipping! Help me, Pa!"

A tear appeared in Creed Taylor's eye as he yelled: "Help's coming, Evie, baby girl!"

ᘒᕲ ᘒᕲ ᘒᕲ ᘒᕲ ᘒᕲ

A heart-rending hour later, running horses approached. It was Amalita, Valencia and Carlos. Carlos sagged in the saddle. The ride had taken much out of him. Pacheco helped him down.

Jason, backing from the hole, filled them in.

"Shaft is real narrow, Mr. Martinez. And there's a little bend. She seems to be just around the bend, about twenty feet down. I could only see one hand. She just slipped a bit further."

Carlos was weak, but drew from some inner strength and spoke firmly to Taylor.

"Creed, I need your two strongest men. Find a long pole and tie a rope in the middle. Your men will hold the pole so that I can go straight down the hole and disturb the dirt as little as possible."

Taylor waved to two of his men. Spotting a downed tree nearby, they grabbed it and began stripping branches. Minutes later, Carlos hung with the rope around his chest. Two men held the pole and Carlos began to descend.

Pacheco held the rope and slowly lowered Carlos. Jason remained at the hole and gave directions.

Small as he was, Carlos could not keep from brushing the sides. Trickles of soil fell. Evie's plaintive cries reached the surface. Creed Taylor stifled a sob. Valencia Martinez came beside him, grasped his arm and spoke softly. "She will be ok, señor. My Carlos is a good man and he will not quit until she is safe."

Creed Taylor looked at her and saw sincerity.

A few minutes later, Jason waved his arm.

"Stop the rope!"

A voice was faintly heard below and Jason spoke again.

"Another foot of rope."

Pacheco eased the rope carefully.

Jason listened and spoke to Pacheco.

"He's there! He's got her! Bring the rope up slowly, Pacheco."

Creed Taylor moved to help Pacheco.

A few minutes later Carlos arose from the hole, one hand extended down, grasping Evie's wrist. Jason quickly grabbed her arm and both Carlos and Evie were over the lip of the hole.

Carlos was bent over, eyes closed and hands on his knees. Evie cried as her father scooped her into his arms. Valencia and Amalita ran to Carlos.

"Carlos!"

He moved feebly and they lowered him to the ground.

Evie moved her head and whispered to her father.

"Mr. Martinez saved me, Pa."

oXo oXo oXo oXo oXo

Two weeks later, Carlos sat in the sun, much improved. Pacheco worked on the corral with Alberto. Valencia was preparing tortillas. Amalita was in the garden. A walking horse was heard and they looked up to see Creed Taylor round the barn. He stopped his horse.

"Ok to ride up, Martinez?"

"Si, Señor Taylor."

Taylor rode up and dismounted, slapping the dust from his trousers and looking uncomfortable. Removing his hat, he nodded to Valencia as she stood by the fire. He glanced at Amalita a long moment and it seemed a corner of his mouth turned upwards. Clearing his throat, he shuffled a moment.

"Martinez...Carlos. I've been real wrong about you. Always been bullheaded, my wife says. You saved my daughter's life. There's not enough I can say to thank you. I guess you might say I've seen the error of my ways... and...well...I'd like it if we could be friends. My hands are working your land right now, driving my stock back to my range."

Carlos approached Taylor and reached out his hand. Taylor grasped it.

"Señor...Creed...I would be honored to be your friend. We are always here for you when you need us."

Creed Taylor sighed.

"Thank you, Carlos. Linder got his walking papers several days ago. And... I was wondering if you might allow me to shoot that gun you bested me with?"

Martinez smiled.

"You are good with a rifle, señor. I think you were nervous that day. You would have won."

Another horse came around the barn. It was Jason. Amalita's eyes brightened. Dismounting and taking hat in hand, Jason nodded to Valencia and approached Carlos.

"Good Day, Mr. Martinez."

"It is indeed a good day, Jason."

Jason cleared his throat.

"Mr. Martinez. I would like your permission to court Amalita."

Carlos grinned.

"You have my permission, Jason. But there are two conditions."

Jason's face showed concern.

"What are they, Sir?"

"First, you must have your father's blessing."

Both looked to Creed, who broke into a big smile.

"She is the finest filly around, Jason. You have my blessing."

Jason grinned as Amalita came beside him.

"The other condition, Sir?"

"The other condition is that you must call me Carlos."

Amalita and Jason smiled at each other.

"Yes, sir…I mean, Carlos."

Carlos looked to both Creed and Jason.

"Valencia has food ready. I would be honored to have you both join us at our table."

Pacheco smiled.

There was peace in the valley.

BLOOD ON THE SADDLE

Bloody fingers clawed the dust, the last act of a man dying a violent and unexpected death. A bystander of philosophical mind wondered to himself whether the claw marks were the struggle of a man seeking to rush into eternity or the desperate fight of a man trying to cling to life and flee the awaiting demons of his just rewards.

Only God – or the Devil – really knew the truth. The exclusive thing visible from this side of the veil was a face and body contorted with the malevolent invasion of a lead slug. In the moments before death, before his chest was ripped open, he momentarily chuckled at the sight of the weapon that fired the bullet. But when it hit, no chuckle remained. In fact, very little remained.

People gasped from the boardwalks, stunned by what they had witnessed. Dilly Joe Johansen dead! Killed by a woman. Most admitted to themselves they were glad he was gone, though. Of course, they said nothing aloud due to the volatility of the dead man's friends.

A rough and crude man, Johansen was known to forsake the business ladies and instead make unwelcome and quite brazen advances on proper ladies.

In a frontier town riding the ragged edge of civilization, it was one thing to approach a woman of obvious profession and make comments and solicit favors. It was quite another thing to bother a woman of more civilized morality. Even Dilly Joe's partners, known as a pack of mangy wolves without concern for anyone whatsoever, tried to keep their distance from his behavior. There was no sheriff to intervene. The last one took a forever nap on boot hill two months back, and none had been brainless enough to take the job since.

There was something about a proper woman that caused a man to think not only of his mother, but of hearth, home and sitting at a table for a home-cooked meal with a child running around. Maybe even going to hear the Sabbath sermon. Out here, ladies were nigh on to sacred. In fact, one circuit-riding parson likened bothering a good woman to pouring wine from the Holy Grail down a snake hole.

Uppity and overconfident, Dilly Joe met his match when he pushed himself on the wrong person. He would certainly never do it again.

Just yards away with her gun facing the pack of wolves, stood the reason Dilly Joe would never bother a woman – any woman – again.

Though deadly with a gun, there was no question the girl known as Maddie was a lady. She was just as comfortable in a dress as in the jeans of the trail. In fact, when she donned a dress there was no hint of anything but woman, for every part of the dress was filled to absolute perfection. And when she wore jeans? Well, suffice it to say that more than one cowboy had misplaced a brand on a piggin-tied calf by letting his eyes wander at the branding fire. It was said that somewhere in Nevada was a calf with a brand on the side of its head. The cowboy never lived it down.

Perhaps because of her beauty, none would guess that this lady also had another name – The Washita Lady. It was a name known only by reputation. None in this town knew her as more than Maddie, a lady who rode in a week ago.

That was part of the problem. Some men thought themselves good judges of such things, and never suspected that within that eye-catching woman was skill with a gun that might make Clay Allison give pause should they happen to meet.

Known for at least four men dead and rumors of others, her identity was sketchy with the variances wrought by rumor and whiskey. It was rumored that Allison mentioned once he might seek her out if only to see if she was as all-fired attractive as some riding the owl-hoot trail claimed.

Right now she dared another to try their hand.

None did.

ↀ ↀ ↀ ↀ ↀ

At a remote campfire that evening, nursing a scalding cup of coffee, Maddie's gut still churned. Her camp was nestled in a jumble of upturned rocks from some ancient trauma to the earth. She had hoped to spend more time in town, but she knew tongues would wag and connections might be made. Within an hour of the shooting, she was on the trail.

In the past four years she had tried to live a quiet life,

but it rarely lasted more than a fortnight or two. Trouble seemed to spring to her like iron to a magnet.

Her real name was Maddie Covington Trapp. Born into Boston high-society, there were misty memories of balls and carriage rides in the park and a nanny tucking her in at night. It all came crashing down when she was just five years old. She knew only that her parents were killed in some sort of fire in a theater, and she remembered standing at the cemetery and then a long train ride with a strange lady. Her uncle met the train in Colorado and she became a part of his family outside of New Haven. Something in Maddie never truly settled. Though loved and provided for, it seemed to others she was always searching for something missing. She didn't participate in idle chatter and tended to be off in her own thoughts much of the time.

As with many frontier families, guns were a part of daily life. Early on, Maddie showed exceptional skill. She delighted in competition and even outshot many grown-ups. Through the years she learned to shoot four-legged varmints with pinpoint accuracy. When she was fifteen, her uncle gave her the .31 Colt she now carried. She practiced steadily in the hills until her skill was beyond what most realized.

Her cousin, Becky, who was fiery and carefree also, and known as an excellent rider, often found Maddie staring out the window towards the west. Whatever was missing in her life caused her to look at the horizon with a wistful anticipation and wanderlust bloomed within her.

One sunny day, as Maddie sat her horse looking over one of the beautiful vistas of the ranch, her uncle rode up the hillside.

"Nice morning, Uncle John."

"It's beautiful, isn't it?"

He watched her for a moment before speaking.

"Maddie, I'm a man of this wide open country. It was quite a bit wilder in those early days. There have been times that I wondered what my life might have been if I'd stayed in Boston and built a profession like your father. But I love the West. I love the wildness, the challenge and the building of a dream. I thoroughly love each new vista and each new trail. I know now that I wouldn't have made it back East. I was not meant for the crowds, the bustle, the noise and the overly settled life. I had to leave and finally settled here. It was where I am meant to be. I see the same restlessness in you, Maddie. You have an unsettled spirit. You had a rough go when your parents died, but I'm not sure that's it. There is just something in you that was meant to wrestle free of the fetters put on us by the conventions of life. You like to see what's over the next hill, and around the next bend in the trail. I don't need to tell you it will be harder for a woman out here than it is for a man. Still, I believe you can do it. I won't stop you when you decide to go your own way. Eventually you will find it and your peace."

"Thanks, Uncle John. I don't understand it all the time, but my heart just isn't content."

"For whatever reason, you're different from other young ladies, Maddie. You've got to find your own way. When that day comes, know that Aunt Betty and most everybody else won't understand. But on that day, you come to me. I won't stop you, but it's important to me that you don't go empty handed."

Maddie stared with love at this man who seemed to understand her better than anyone else.

"Maddie, you've got an unusual skill with that gun. I've seen men with great skill, and you're right up there with them. It's still a dangerous land. Remember that many men will act like they want to help, but what they want is to help themselves. Up till now you have shot only four-legged varmints. You mind my words that you're gonna run into the two-legged kind sooner or later. There'll be many who will think they can take advantage of a woman alone. You'll know the type and you best not give them any opportunities. Never, ever give up your gun. Be wise, but don't hesitate to protect yourself."

The day came when Maddie rode off, turning in the saddle to look back once more upon the ranch. That morning, when she walked up to her Uncle, he saw the look in her eyes and knew. His eyes moistened a little as he went to his room and brought her a wallet of mixed paper money and trickled some gold coins into her palm.

"Careful with the jingling sound gold makes. People hear it when they can't hear anything else. Keep only what you need in your pocket and best act like you're mostly broke. Don't back down from a righteous cause. Always hold your head up and don't do anything that makes you do otherwise. And take care of that gun. Mind what I said about two-legged varmints." He reached into his pocket. "Here's a derringer. It belonged to your father. Always keep it within easy reach. And wire us now and then to let us know you're all right. You will be in our thoughts and prayers."

"I'll remember, Uncle John. I'm not going to say goodbye to the others. You understand. Please tell them all how much they mean to me."

The truth of his words came sooner than she expected. Maddie was waylaid on the road a month later by a man who took her womanhood for weakness. He had a malicious grin and moved for her. She shot him through the third shirt button and stood for a long time looking down at him and fighting the turmoil inside her. Not wanting to be falsely accused, Maddie rode off, leaving an unsigned note on the dead man's shirt telling her side of the story. It was called, for whatever reason, the Washita Road, and the mystery of the Washita Lady began. When the unexplained, mysterious, times a bad man disappeared – people would look solemn and nod. Nobody really knew, but all presumed it was the Washita Lady. Nobody knew who she was, but everybody knew her handiwork. Or so they thought. In reality, most instances had nothing to do with her. Most anyway.

A few weeks later, Maddie happened upon a bank robbery. One outlaw tried to take a little girl hostage. Maddie heard the ruckus and saw his intent. Seeing a beautiful woman confronting him, he hesitated. Maddie did not.

Boot hill gained another tenant and Maddie was a hero. She stayed a few days, but the attention was troublesome. So Maddie headed west on a faint game trail, needful of being away.

Amidst the quiet travel, there were the occasional stops when she'd run into some situation that needed resolution by lead. She didn't want to kill. It was just that on the edge of the frontier things were handled differently.

She heard a hoof clip rock in the darkness and slipped into the rocks.

ᚱᚾ ᚱᚾ ᚱᚾ ᚱᚾ ᚱᚾ

A lone horse, blood smeared on the saddle, wandered nervously into camp. Slipping from the darkness, Maddie spoke softly to the horse. It started to shy away, but the comfort of the fire and the instinctive sense of a beast for the gentleness of her words caused it to pause. Hands rubbing its mane, the horse nickered.

"What is it, fella? Where's the man who rode you?"

The blood was still wet. Somewhere out there, likely close, was a man wounded or worse. She spoke quietly to herself.

"Maddie, you left the frying pan and it seems you're going to jump right into the fire." She led the horse back the way it had come, walking to see the hoof prints easier in the subtle light of the waning moon.

It was a slow half hour later when the horse slowed and she heard a soft moan. He lay at the base of an upthrust crag of rock. Blood covered his shirtfront, originating low on the left side.

"Doggone, mister. Looks like you caught a bad one. But it might not be the end of you yet. We need to get you some help."

The man's eyes flicked open briefly, then rolled shut. Sliding him on the blanket she found behind his saddle, she tied the corners to the horn with rope and turned them back to camp.

∽∾ ∽∾ ∽∾ ∽∾ ∽∾

Maddie had been around ranch hands enough to hear stories of such wounds, and actually saw a couple herself. It was clear the bullet had gone through, so she washed and bound the wounds. She recalled the lessons of one old cow-hand who told her one never knew whether such wounds were clean or if the bullet did a switchback or two while traveling through. Only time would tell. Rest was crucial. That and water.

Maddie spent the night restless and listening to the darkness, pausing now and then to wipe the man's brow. Shortly after midnight he opened his eyes and glanced around. He caught site of Maddie and a question crossed his brow.

"How did I get here and who are you?"

"You've been hit pretty bad, mister. Best lay still. My name is Maddie."

The man struggled to speak.

"Name's Ross. Ross Davis."

"Who shot you?"

"Taggart Johansen. He'll try to find me to make sure he did the job right."

"Why'd he want you dead?"

"Because they're rustling cattle. They run the Double-B. Stealing from other outfits, but mainly from the 88 up north. Taggart and his brothers, Luther and Dilly Joe, will be out here to make sure I'm dead."

"Dilly Joe won't be bothering you."

"Why's that?"

"Dead. Back down the road a piece."

"Known to be fast with a gun."

"Not fast enough."

Ross looked for a few moments at Maddie.

"That'll rile Luther something awful."

"You picked the wrong crowd to mess with, Davis." Maddie saw her horse's head jerk up and look outward. "Don't make a sound."

Slipping quietly through the rocks, Maddie hugged a boulder and strained her ears to the darkness. Something was out there. All her senses warned her of danger. She remained still and waited. Oftentimes, the dead in this country were those who could not wait, who ventured carelessly into the darkness. Even on dark nights, a man – or woman – could be outlined against a lighter background. Any movement attracted the eyes. So she waited.

Off to the left there was a subtle rattle of gravel. She turned her eyes only and saw a movement in the dark, about thirty yards away. A man was circling.

She heard a chuckle, then a soft voice.

"I know you're out there. Who are you?"

Maddie remained silent. If there were another man out there, his goal would be to get her to respond in order to locate her. She remained silent, listening.

"We're looking for a wounded friend."

Off to her right was a faint brush of cloth against rock. She knew the first man would move just a bit to keep her guessing. Maddie tensed.

"We're mighty grateful of your care. But he needs more than campfire doctoring." She could hear the smirk in his voice.

Hearing sound mere feet away, she slammed her gun barrel up and sideways.

A grunt of pain was followed by the sound of a man falling. In the dark she saw his eyes wide and his hands grasping at his jaw. Maddie cocked her Colt and pointed it directly at the man's head while talking plainly into the dark.

"I don't know who you are, but you are either Luther or Taggart. I have my pistol at the face of your brother. He will die if I don't hear your voice fading and a horse riding away. And I want to hear you singing as you ride off."

"A woman! Just who might you be?"

"A woman who can take care of herself and...shoot your brother without mercy just like you shot that rider."

The man beside her spoke up. It was difficult with the damage to his jaw.

"Tag! She'll do it. Don't do nothin' foolish!"

So this was Luther she had at gunpoint.

"Ok, I'm leaving. What about Luther?"

"I'll tie him to his saddle and send him along later."

"This ain't going to end it, lady. Taggart Johansen doesn't back down. We'll meet again. From the sound of your voice, you must be a young thing." The tone was not good.

An hour later she listened as Luther and his horse faded into the distance. She rigged a travois with Davis' mount and headed out the back way. It would be impossible to cover all their tracks, so Maddie took care to take a route over rocks and hard ground. It would be rougher on Davis, but that couldn't be helped.

ᵒᵀᵒ ᵒᵀᵒ ᵒᵀᵒ ᵒᵀᵒ ᵒᵀᵒ

The next morning, they stopped to let the horses rest. Ross told Maddie that the 88 brand was registered to old man Saunders. He lived up against the mountains with his ten-year-old grandson, Val. The boy's father was killed a couple months earlier in town in a gunfight with Taggart Johansen over the fact that the Double-B brand fit perfectly over the 88. The sheriff attempted to arrest Taggart for murder, but died himself, and Taggart declared publicly both were fair fights. Nobody argued and Taggart and Luther and Dilly Joe had their way after that.

Saunders' herds began to thin, and his three hands were beaten and threatened by men of the Double-B. None of the hands were fighters and asked for their time and drifted. Now it was just old man Saunders and Val, and the Johansen's slowly sorted the cattle and rebranded. Cattle had been disappearing by the dozens. Saunders, an old catamount with more than enough guts, wanted to take the fight to the enemy, but he needed to protect Val.

Ross Davis rode in one day and shared a meal with Saunders, declaring the biscuits as good as any woman's, and the laughter formed a bond. Saunders explained and Ross, though not a gunman, was familiar with the issues at hand. He decided life held nothing urgent and stuck around. On his way back from sending a telegram for Saunders, he was ambushed by the Johansen's. No warning was given.

Maddie shook her head.

"And no law around to help."

Davis winced with pain.

"Nobody. And Saunders is willing to fight, but he wants no harm to his grandson."

"The telegram?"

"To some fella he knows up north. Said he was a friend."

Maddie stood and looked around.

"Well, we're headed to the 88. Got to get you in bed and doctor those wounds. You've lost a lot of blood, but I don't think you're torn up too much. Time and care should do it."

"There ain't much time for Saunders. He'll be washed up before long."

"We'll see."

ᚨᚨ ᚨᚨ ᚨᚨ ᚨᚨ ᚨᚨ

Just a few days north, at the dusty end of a cattle drive, an old man sat with friends in the trail-end town. They were friends he saw every couple years when he rode through. Laughing and trading lies with each other, they glanced up as the telegraph operator walked in, grabbed a drink and joined them. He looked to the old man.

"Funny how it works sometimes."

"How what works?"

"How I pass messages up and down the telegraph lines. Sometimes they come for local folks and I can't find them for nothing. Then along comes a telegram for someone who only shows up every whip-stitch and I can pass it on right away."

He handed over a sheet of paper. The old man read it and a grave look crossed his face. He rose from his seat.

"Gotta pack my gear, fellas. A friend a bit south of here wants me to drop in. Needful of my help."

"Daggone. At least finish your beer."

He reached down and drained the glass and brushed his sleeve across his mouth.

"Love to visit with you mangy dogs, but I'm leaving tonight."

❖ ❖ ❖ ❖ ❖

Ross Davis was abed for three days before he ventured out of the small but solid ranch house. He was just in time to see Maddie ride in. Saunders came from the barn to meet her.

"See anything?"

"Cattle being bunched at a couple places two, three hours away. I suspect they've got a valley filled with your stock and plan a drive. Not seeing but a few of your herd still loose. Johansen's working pretty hard."

Val came up to his grandfather. "Gramps? There's a rider coming."

Eyes turned to see the man in the distance.

Maddie squinted. The rider was indistinguishable.

Saunders looked at Val. "Best go inside, Val." The boy walked to the house and stood just inside the door, reaching for the Winchester that rested there.

Davis spoke from where he leaned against the logs of the house. "Expecting anybody, Saunders?"

"Might be. But not this soon. Can't rightly make him out."

They all stared intently, with Maddie turning to scan other directions. It would not be beyond the Johansens to create a distraction while others snuck up from behind. But there was nobody in sight.

Saunders took a few steps forward and strained. Then he smiled.

"Well, I'll be…"

Maddie looked over. "Friend?"

"Yep."

The rider walked his horse into the ranch yard. His clothes were trail worn. Obviously older than Saunders, he looked tough and sinewy. There was friendliness in his eyes. But something said he was quite capable and not one to mess with. At his hip was a LeMat 9-shot revolver with a central barrel holding a 20-gauge shotgun shell. It was not a common weapon. He looked at Saunders and grinned. "Saunders, good to see you, old friend!"

"Same to you, Skerby! Light and set."

જ⁘ જ⁘ જ⁘ જ⁘ જ⁘

Skerby drained the last swig of his coffee.

"Seen them driving fresh-branded Double-B's right

through town. Not even branded well. Just like they was daring you to say something."

Saunders nodded. "They want me to challenge them so they can shoot me down to get me out of the way. They'll set me up and catch me in a crossfire."

Maddie drank her coffee. "That's why we haven't seen them on the range and they haven't attacked here. No need. They know you'll have to do something or be stolen blind. They know Ross is down for a bit and unable to help."

Ross stepped into the room.

"I can handle a long gun ok."

Saunders looked at Val, but spoke to the group. "Val keeps me going now. He's the spittin' image of his pa. And he's handy with a Winchester."

Skerby got up and refilled his cup. "So, we got to have a plan they won't think of." He looked at Saunders. "They're bunching the cattle. Gonna drive them. Been a rough year back East and beef are selling for high dollar and going fast. My guess is they'll try and make a quick deal and go find greener pastures after a bit of partying. There are buyers just north of here, a weeks' drive. They have their own crews to drive the herds to the railhead. Buying close keeps the costs down. They pay less per head, but the ranchers don't have the expense of a long drive. I think that's what the Johansen's will do."

Saunders agreed. "I think you're right, Skerby. And they think they've got us bottled up here. Probably try and start something just before the drive to keep us from riding out. We ain't seen any sign of them close lately."

Maddie spoke, "Skerby and I should hide out in the

hills until something happens."

"Maddie, this ain't your fight." Saunders said. "You just hightail it out of here and stay clear."

"I've been raised different than that. When I was growing up, my uncle who raised me used to say, 'Once you jump into a ruckus, you don't leave till the ruckus is over.' So I'm going nowhere."

Skerby's eyes jumped suddenly to Maddie, and he raised an eyebrow.

Saunders spoke up. "But this ain't no fight for a young woman."

"I can handle myself…don't judge a book by it's cover."

"Well, it goes against the grain a mite, though. But I reckon I'm beholden to you. Skerby, I never expected you to be here so quick, and it sounds like just a matter of days before it all comes down. No time for much scouting or sending for other help."

Skerby grinned at Saunders and chuckled.

"Sometimes it don't take as many as you think. Sometimes a small army's all it takes – if'n you got the right folks riding."

❧ ❧ ❧ ❧ ❧

Maddie and Skerby left after dark, carefully avoiding locations an observer might choose. They wanted to get close to the cattle and watch what happened. The rustlers took no pains to hide the trail, which stood out even in the night. It was after midnight when they stopped in a small but deep ravine. There was enough grass for the horses and a place to build a small fire with little risk of prying eyes.

"I 'spect we'll find the herd not too many miles ahead. They won't want to move them too far off the trail." Skerby looked at Maddie, who had gathered a few twigs and put the coffee on. "I ain't gonna pry, but you carry that Colt like it's downright comfortable. That's rare for a young lady."

"I don't go looking for trouble."

"Weren't saying that. But you look like you don't run from it, neither. I knowed a lot of women could handle a gun near as well as anybody. Heard of others – like this Washita Lady. Reputation, but nobody knows who she is. Interesting, that saying you learned from your uncle. 'Bout the ruckus. I heard that before. From a man up north name of Trapp."

There was a perceptible flash in Maddie's eyes.

Skerby chuckled. "He was trying to pass the word there was need for this Maddie to contact him. Something about back East and a will. It was all-fired important. Might be good to get hold of him."

Maddie stiffened but glanced firmly at Skerby.

"Message received."

"Don't you fret, girl. I ain't gonna tell nothin' to nobody. I reckon I got no worries about your being able to handle a shootin' iron. But these other fella's be shooting back. That's a whole 'nother thing."

"I've faced that before, Skerby. You don't have to worry about me."

Skerby looked Maddie in the eyes and read from their depths.

"I reckon I don't. Don't have to worry none at all."

❦ ❦ ❦ ❦ ❦

It was early the next afternoon when they spotted two riders heading towards the ranch and knew it was beginning. Skerby and Maddie circled and came to the edge of a valley and found a large herd. Riders were working in the distance and the cattle were bunched and ready to drive.

Dry camping that night, Skerby and Maddie watched the men below sit around the fire, laughing and passing a bottle.

The drive began in the morning. They wondered what was going on at the ranch, but their job was to confirm the direction of the herd and meet up later with Saunders. With only two men sent to pin down Saunders, the Johansen's must believe there was little threat there.

❦ ❦ ❦ ❦ ❦

When the first shot plowed into the doorjamb, Saunders was outside. Diving for cover behind a barrel at the corner of the house, he looked to the barn where Val was feeding the horses. He saw Val peering around the corner. Saunders spoke to his grandson in a quiet tone so as not to be overheard.

"Val, stay in the barn. Stay out of sight. Don't come out for any reason until I tell you it's ok. An' I tucked a few pieces of jerky in my saddlebags on the wall."

"Ok, Gramps."

"And there's a Winchester in the tack box."

Saunders then turned to the house.

"Ross?"

"Yes?"

"You count a slow ten seconds and swing that door wide. I'm coming in." On the count, he made a diving run through the door as a bullet plowed dirt at his feet. "May be a long day. Keep shy of the door."

All day long, sporadic shots hit the house. Obviously, the attackers figured all of them were in the house. It became clear they were sent to keep Saunders pinned down.

Come dark, Saunders slipped out through the shadows and worked his way to the barn. He brought Val to the house, where they ate together in the dark. Saunders packed his saddlebags.

"Val, I ain't sayin' it's gonna happen, but part of growing up out here requires being able to shoot in mighty unpleasant situations. You know what I'm sayin' to ya?"

"I know, Gramps. One of those men shot Pa."

"That's a fact, boy. Now you and Davis are holding the home."

☙❧ ☙❧ ☙❧ ☙❧ ☙❧

The next day, Saunders rounded a bend in the brush and joined Skerby and Maddie. Determination showed in their faces as they turned and headed north.

Just days later, Taggart Johansen rode into the town, a couple men with him. The drive had been quick and without issues and he was eager to make a quick deal and get out.

Asking directions, he rode to the hotel and went in. A man in Eastern clothing sat with a group of men. Taggart walked up confidently.

"Name's Johansen. Got a herd south of town. Thousand head of prime beef. Where do I find a buyer?"

One of the men stood up.

"I'm Pickering, got a drive heading to market in a couple days."

"I'm sellin' for whoever gives the best price."

The doors opened and closed behind Johansen. An old man and a young woman stepped in and to the side. The two men with Johansen glanced over briefly and turned back to Taggart.

Pickering glanced over at the newcomers. He grinned.

"Skerby! You old no-account! What are you doing here?"

"Came to sell cattle, Pick. Thousand head."

Taggart Johansen turned angrily. "Mister, I'm here ahead of you. Wait your turn."

Pickering spoke sharply. "Johansen, I'm the only market for all the cattle that come in. Hold your temper."

Taggart flushed as Pickering turned to Skerby.

"How many you got, Skerby?"

"Thousand head."

"I know you well enough, Skerby. Give you twenty-three dollars a head, gold."

"Deal, Pick. They's bunched south of town."

Taggart Johansen turned and spluttered, "Ain't no

cows south of here but ours."

"I don't know what's happened, but them's Saunders cows out there."

"They're my brand – the Double-B. I got the papers."

"Might be Double-B on the outside, but skin one and I think you'll see the original brand is an 88. That's Saunders' brand. Got the papers. Somebody ripped you off."

Pickering knew trouble when he saw it. The other men sat without moving. Taggart slowly turned to face Skerby.

"You calling me a liar?"

Maddie stepped forward a pace. "He's not, but I am."

Taggart's eyes widened. "Do I know you, little lady?"

"Yep. Luther's carrying my mark, and Dilly Joe's pushin' up daisies."

Taggart Johansen cursed and reached for his gun. The men said later that Maddie's hand was a blur. A split second later, Taggart toppled to the ground. The other two men froze. Skerby kept them covered.

Pickering sent word to the sheriff, who gathered a quick posse to get the other rustler's, but either a sixth sense or slipped word reached them first and they headed to the hills, where they were seen splitting in all directions. It would be almost impossible to get them.

❧❧ ❧❧ ❧❧ ❧❧ ❧❧

Maddie, Skerby and Saunders sat that evening in the restaurant. They were exhausted. They knew Davis and Val were stuck in the ranch house. They would head back after finishing their meal.

Quiet from the happenings of the day, they made a bit of small talk.

They were waiting for what they knew must come.

At the livery, they saddled their horses and turned to lead them out the door.

Luther Johansen stood in the doorway, gun in hand. He had a wild look in his eye.

"You think you won? My brothers are dead and I demand life for life."

Saunders looked at him. "Which of you Johansen's killed my son?"

"I did. And boy was it easy."

Saunders clawed at his pistol and Luther fired, too soon. As the slug tore Saunders' sole off his boot, Maddie fired, hitting Luther in the shoulder. Luther stumbled, then stood and started to lift his gun again when Skerby let loose with the 20 gauge barrel of the LaMat. Luther flew backwards against the wall and slipped lifeless to the floor.

❦ ❦ ❦ ❦ ❦

At a fork in the trail, Maddie pulled up and looked from one to the other in the moonlight.

"What's wrong, Maddie?" Saunders looked around.

"This is as far as I go. I'm headed east."

"You don't have to go. There's a home for you here."

"I appreciate it, Saunders, but I have something I need to do."

Saunders looked at her with a question in his eyes.

"But…well, Maddie, I guess I got to understand. But

you mind the door is always open for you. Day or night."

"Thanks, and give my best to Val and Davis."

Skerby, silent until now, tilted his head. "Might be I know somebody would want to know you're ok."

Maddie smiled. "They'll know soon enough, Skerby. And I thank you."

The station attendant looked twice at the beautiful young lady buying the ticket for Boston. Earlier, she had sent a wire to her Uncle John.

Conversation stopped among the handful of cowhands getting ready to board the train. They tipped their hats to her and tried to hide their furtive glances. Maddie smiled to herself.

She settled on a bench and placed her carpetbag at her feet. Conversation soon resumed.

"I heard it from a man what's been on the trail!"

"It couldn't be the Washita Lady! She's in California. Hear tell she's got blazing red hair."

"I heard she's in Wyoming. And hair black as a raven. Nose about as long as a beak!"

"I got it from a man claims to have seen her. All gray and wrinkled. Said she's ugly as sin!"

"Might gotta be to shoot that good. Probably looks like a man."

They hooted.

"I heard she's dead. Kilt in a fight down north of Sonora."

Maddie kept a straight face.

A train whistle sounded in the distance.

Sighing, she nudged her carpetbag with her toe, assuring herself of the presence, deep within, of the .31 Colt and holster.

She would not need it this trip – hopefully. Reaching to her pocket, she felt the comforting presence of her father's derringer. It was a part of her now.

Besides, one never knew when the Washita Lady would rise again.

THE GRIZZLY BEAR

Death was a natural part of life on the frontier. That said, most men preferred not to participate.

Leet Stone knew death from close up. His first exposure was his mother. Standing, hat in hand and tears welling, he watched her quilt-wrapped body lowered into a lonely grave on the hillside overlooking the hard-scrabble good-for-nothing piece of ground that killed her. His second exposure to death was his father who, senseless with corn whiskey, picked a fight with the wrong man and was cruelly beaten to death.

Death had many fingers. One of those fingers was the banker coming to the cabin the day after his father's funeral. Leet, only fifteen but wise in the ways of the world, noted the man's smiling eyes as he spoke from horseback.

"Boy, you can't make the payments on this place, so you got to get out." Looking around, the man knew the cabin was well built. Leet could see greed in his eyes. "Now, I'm a sensitive man to what you been through, so I'll give you two days to leave."

Leet merely nodded. A day later he rode out on an old sway-backed mule with all that mattered in his life tucked in his saddlebags and tied to the cantle. Behind him the cabin and barn gave their all to the fires he set. Leet would see no man profit from his loss – much less get pleasure from it. His last glance was to the matching graves upon the hillside. Giving a silent wave, he turned his head to the west and never looked back.

Twenty-five years had passed since he burned the banker's smile, and life had not been easy. A succession of jobs kept him in the necessaries, but none held any future other than a bit of jingling in his pocket. Over the years he'd felt a growing wish to find some place and just…stay. And be left alone.

Now he stood at a simple bar in a town that would one day be forgotten.

He didn't have to look to know they stared. They always did. When he walked in, conversations stopped and were followed by the usual whispering and pointing. It was routine.

Because of the lumbering walk of a man in no real hurry, some bystanders made the assumption that he was slow and stupid. He was neither slow nor stupid – but he stood out in any crowd. Leet was different enough from others that anonymity was never an option. As opposite from his father as he could be, Leet was a muscled bulk of a man, though not all lean. At just shy of six-foot, his starting-to-be-prominent stomach was held in check with a subtle tug of the worn and strained brass button of his canvas trousers and the stout leather braces over his shoulders. His hands were large and thick and scars crossed his knuckles from unavoidable altercations.

Incredibly thick whiskers, starting to gray and growing like corn in perfect Iowa weather, covered his face and did not stop at his neckline. Those rare individuals who saw him without a shirt stared in awe, whistled and muttered comments about bearskins. Indeed, when Leet scraped his whiskers every few days in an attempt to look civilized, it seemed like mere hours later that the effort had been worthless.

Hair hung to his shoulders and curled over his collar. Peaceful yet wary eyes peered from beneath bushy eyebrows that one wide-eyed child shying from him called "winter wooly worms." Under one brow was a scar running across the eyelid and almost to his ear. Done by a renegade knife, the original owner needed the blade no more and Leet carried it tied down the back of his neck. A precaution.

His sheer size invited challenge and many an unwanted fight was pressed on him, usually by a local tough egged on by others too chicken to take the task on themselves. The way Leet figured it, if the fights were inevitable, he might as well win. Over the years he learned the ways of scrapping, fair and unfair, and used what best seemed to fit the occasion.

Leet stared at the glass before him.

A man given to manners when they rightfully belonged, Leet thought often of his mother and the manners she instilled in his youth. Keeping them was a remembrance of her. Still, there were times when situations required a different method and he did what circumstance required. Prone to deep thought, with many long hours alone on horseback and in remote line cabins, Leet had worn out the pages of many books. His knowledge surpassed that of many men of the frontier.

His size itself was misleading. The bulk belied a stunning quickness in both the palming of a gun and straight-arming once unbroken jaws.

Though many a used gun could be had, Leet Stone's .45 was neither pristine nor worn out. Used only for necessity, he sought to live life without its persuasive capacities.

Problem was, varmints came in many shapes and sizes. And they'd filled his life. He just attracted them. More than once he turned his eyes heavenward and prayed for a different life.

Leet sighed now, hearing a man strutting toward him.

Leet was disappointed. He just wanted peace and a lingering moment over his drink.

Doggone varmints.

"Hey, Grizzly! What cave you come from?"

Chuckling erupted from a nearby table. The speaker had friends. Like a den of coyotes, Leet thought as he stared at the bar.

A voice from the den was tinged with laughter.

"He don't hear you, Grady. Probably fresh from hibernation."

More chuckles.

Leet flexed his fingers. He knew where this was headed. Why wait?

"Boys, look at the pelt on this beast!"

More chuckles. The man was close.

"Grady, that rug would look good on the floor of your cabin. Give the dog something to curl up on."

Leet took another sip of his drink.

"Hey, Mr. Bear! You been asleep in your cave?"

Going by the sound, Leet turned with lightning speed and the pile driver of his fist dropped the man instantly to the floor. With one fluid motion, Leet's hand dropped and palmed his .45 while the den of coyotes still stared with shock.

"Anybody else want trouble, or can I finish my drink?"

Silence. Turning, Leet Stone laid the pistol near to hand and returned to his drink.

So much for the desire of a quiet night in town after a long dusty ride.

The man named Grady lay still, but the fact his nose was smashed was obvious.

"Mister, we need to get Grady to a doctor. He's in bad shape."

"Leave him. A man ought to have a chance to think about his mistakes. When I leave, do as you please."

Nobody argued.

๛ ๛ ๛ ๛ ๛

The chicken was as tasty as he'd ever had in any frontier town. The waitress, a mite careworn and probably pushing thirty, gave him a smile. It was as if she didn't see or react to his appearance. Her eyes showed only kindness.

"More coffee?"

"Yes, please, ma'am."

Her eyes flickered to his after he spoke. There was a question in their depths. It remained unasked, as were so many questions on the frontier where privacy and the past were respected.

Wiping his hands on the napkin, he carefully folded it and laid it beside the plate. Glancing up, he caught her staring. She looked down in embarrassment, paused, and then came to the table.

"I'm sorry for staring." She paused. "It's just that you have manners and I don't see it so often. Especially…" She blushed.

"Especially in a Grizzly bear?"

Eyes wide, she was about to turn away when he chuckled.

"Ma'am. I meant no offense. I'm used to the term."

She looked at him for a long moment, and then laughed. It was a light and refreshing laugh. His heart lifted.

"I meant no offense, either."

"I go by Leet. Leet Stone. And the manners come from my mother. She always quoted the scripture that said, 'Train up a child in the way which he should go, and when he is old he will not depart from it.' I guess it worked. Many men may look wild but inside are more refined than first glance would show." He looked to the ceiling, quizzically. "And then there are the others, of course."

She smiled and topped off his cup. Leet noted the calluses. Working hands.

"Carrie Larsen."

Leet lingered a moment as he gently grasped her small hand.

"You lived here long, Carrie?"

"About ten years."

"Got a farm?"

"What makes you ask…?" She paused and looked at

her hands and put them in her apron pocket. The smile left her face and sadness, mixed with anger, took its place. "I had a farm. And a husband. Flash flood took my husband. The banker, Simpson Collier, took my farm a month ago."

Memories of long ago filled Leet's mind. Memories of his younger self riding away from burning buildings. And the graves upon the hillside.

"Why'd the banker take it?" He asked.

"Said I couldn't run the whole outfit. I tried, but I couldn't find anyone to help. He wants every ranch around. His men push away or threaten – or pistol whip – anyone who gets in his way. He had his men move all my belongings to the dirt outside the door. I got the most important things, but now here I am."

"Yet you're still cheerful?"

"Mister – Leet, I got a strong faith in God. I know He'll take care of me. My misfortune isn't any reason to foist my loss upon others. Besides, I truly love people."

"Where do you live now?"

"A little room above the kitchen."

"No kids?"

"No." A wistfulness crossed her face, but quickly vanished.

"How long since your husband died?"

"Nigh on to a year now."

She smiled.

"Why the smile?"

"Because Grady is one of Simpson Collier's thugs. You handled him with, shall we say, a firm hand? Besides, Grady was at the farm and threw my belongings into the yard." A chuckle caused her to raise a hand to her mouth and look around.

Leet smiled.

"It don't take long for news to spread, does it?"

"I imagine Mr. Collier is a bit put out right about now. And I suspect you will be meeting him. He knows how things work. There isn't much to talk about in town. Besides, a lot of people are smiling behind drawn curtains for what you did. He knows that." She looked around. The dining room was empty. "There's those here in town and about the territory who are up against Simpson Collier now. Some have been given notice. He'll do anything to get hold of the land. If he died today, there would be a lot of people at the funeral. But it would be to spit on his grave."

Leet's bushy eyebrows raised.

"Somehow I don't think you'd be among those spitting."

Carrie grinned.

"No, I know he's done wrong, but I wouldn't stoop so low."

Leet paused, then reached to his pocket. Pulling out a handful of coins, he paid for his meal, then handed her a twenty-dollar gold piece as a tip.

"Thanks for giving a good meal and a smile to a man not used to it." Why he said his next words, he didn't know. "You're a mighty fine looking lady." He reddened.

Carrie blushed also, but not in anger. She smiled.

"Breakfast is served at six."

❧ ❧ ❧ ❧ ❧

A man leaned against the corner of the building across from the hotel. There was no attempt to hide the glow of his cigarette in the darkness. Ordered to watch the stranger, he failed to think he might be watched himself.

He was.

Leet Stone did not like being watched. In fact, it angered him. Letting the curtain corner gently fall, he slipped his boots on.

Ten minutes later the watcher felt a tap on his shoulder. Startled, he turned to see a large shadow, then felt the blow from Leet's fist. Tied securely with old rope, he did not awaken till morning.

Leet slept peacefully.

❧ ❧ ❧ ❧ ❧

Breakfast was busy. Carrie did not have time to talk, but did make sure Leet's coffee never got cold.

A portly, well-dressed man came in precisely at 8 a.m. as Carrie filled Leet's cup. Leet sensed the change in her as the door opened and she looked up. Glancing back at Leet, the change told him all he needed to know. Another man followed and stood inside the door, clearly along to be the tough man if needed. Surveying the room, the man rested his eyes on Leet, who met his gaze calmly and held it until the man looked away.

The man walked to his usual table and sat.

Simpson Collier.

Watching him, Leet was quick to realize the man wanted to be treated as better than others. His Prince

Albert coat was well made and a gold watch chain crossed the ample mid section. Wispy side-whiskers made a pitiful attempt to mimic muttonchops. Fat fingers reached up to carefully curry his hair, which was parted in the middle and plastered with tonic.

Some others in the dining room left, meals unfinished. One, Leet noticed, had just received his breakfast, but then just slipped out while casting a sideways glance at Collier.

Leet focused on his breakfast. He was sure Carrie had brought him extra and it had been weeks since he'd had anything but jerky for breakfast.

Jotting notes with pencil and paper, Collier rarely looked up except when someone walked in or departed. Whenever his coffee was not kept filled, Collier snapped his fingers and set the cup noisily on the edge of the table.

Leet wondered what made a man turn into what this man was. There were all sorts of possibilities, but sometimes a man was just born a coyote and preying on others was in the breeding. Collier conveyed an air of superiority, expecting deference.

Collier's eyes lifted and caught Leet's apprising eyes. Leet did not flinch or look away. Backing down was not in his nature. The banker looked down, then up again. Setting his pencil down, he glared at Leet.

"What are you looking at?"

"Not much." It was abrupt, but the man already irked him.

Carrie heard the words and snickered, a sound not unnoticed by Simpson Collier. Anger flickered across the man's eyes and his mouth tightened.

"Mister, you annoy me."

"I been told that before."

Carrie sat a plate in front of Collier, filled his coffee and walked away. Collier said nothing and, instead, glanced lewdly at her figure as she walked to the kitchen. Leet was irritated as the man's eyes lingered.

But what business was this of his? The best thing to do would be to finish breakfast, saddle his horse and ride out.

Carrie appeared at his side, refilling his cup. She lipped the word "careful" to him.

Collier dug into his food with relish. Leet finished his meal and lingered over coffee. Collier finally put down his fork, looked around and put his notes in his coat pocket. He looked directly at Leet.

"Maybe you should see a barber before you go back to whatever – cave – you came from."

"Collier, you seem mighty confident."

"I see you already know who I am." He spoke smugly and looked to make sure others heard. "And judging by the description, you must be the 'Grizzly bear' that laid out my man Grady."

"The man was not too polite."

"I assure you, Mr...?"

"Stone."

"I assure you, Mr. Stone, your presence in this town is unwanted. I presume you will be leaving...soon?"

"Not sure. I might stay a spell."

"I would suggest not." He looked around once again to make sure others were listening. They were, for such an interchange would be around town quickly. "In fact, I would suggest your breakfast would digest better in the saddle."

Leet stared, a touch of anger mixed with humor in his eyes.

Collier gripped his cup and paused.

"A man was found tied up in the livery barn this morning. I understand he showed signs of…er…being struck."

Leet took a sip of his coffee and spoke sharply.

"Struck from the front or the back?"

"What difference does it make?"

"It tells whether the man who hit him was afraid or not."

Simpson Collier paused, then looked to his watch and stood, carefully counting out exact change for his meal and dropping them roughly to the table. Leaving no tip for Carrie, he strode out without a further glance. The man at the door merely stepped into stride behind him.

Carrie wandered over with the coffee.

"You didn't make a friend."

"Wasn't my intention."

"He's a big man in town, Leet."

"The bigger they are, the harder they fall."

"So there was a second man last night? You're creating a stir, Leet."

"Man's got a right to be left alone."

"You going to leave?"

Did he sense sadness in the question? He looked to the door, then to Carrie. She really was an attractive lady with a deep strength inside. To lose the farm to that man and then politely serve him breakfast spoke of something unique.

"If I planned to leave, I certainly can't now. People would think it was because I feared Collier. It'd make him even bigger." Leet looked thoughtful. "I guess I don't mind him being bigger so much as me being seen as smaller. Sort of gets a man's pride. No, I'm staying for a mite."

❧❧ ❧❧ ❧❧ ❧❧ ❧❧

With no specific task at hand, Leet took a ride in the countryside. Carrie gave him a general description and he explored, finally arriving at the farm Collier stole from her.

Not a bad piece of land, he thought. Carrie's husband had a good eye for quality. He smiled as he pictured Carrie's face. The cabin was well placed for both defense and proximity to water. The man also knew the value of a view to a woman glancing out a kitchen window.

Leet watched - and he waited.

Glancing carefully behind, he sighed with satisfaction.

All morning long he knew he was followed. At his last stop, carefully building a small fire, he took out his small camp pot and made coffee. Then he doused the fire and rode off, leaving the pot – along with a surprise.

No sign of the rider again behind him assured his success. Now he waited out of spite and a wry sense of humor. Dismounting, he tied his horse and found a shade tree.

Awakening an hour later, he headed back. More than once, he pulled into trees as riders passed, pushing cows.

Collier's men, no doubt. But likely not his cattle.

He heard the man whimpering before he saw him. Leet began to whistle a carefree tune. It brought the expected result.

"Help!"

The voice was labored and desperate.

Leet grinned and rode into the trees, spotting his coffee pot – still sitting on the rocks where he left it. Above, hanging upside down was a man with a red and swollen head.

Leet sat his horse and looked at the man.

"Howdy."

"Help."

"Oh, I guess you might be a mite uncomfortable. Pardon my not noticing."

"Cut me down." The man was straining to speak.

"Bet you got a headache. Sometimes curiosity can give a man a headache."

"Please…cut me down."

"Well, doggone it, you have a touch of manners."

Dismounting, Leet gathered a few sticks and kindled a fire, moving the pot to take the heat. Then, reaching to his saddlebag and pulling out his cup, he squatted where he could look the distressed man in the face.

"Collier pay you much?"

"Please cut me down."

"I'll give it some thought…if you answer me."

"Collier don't pay enough."

"You plan to collect your wages and leave the area?"

"It's in my mind."

"I wouldn't find it kindly to see you again. Sort of irritates me to have someone follow me."

"Cut me down and I'm leaving."

Leet kicked the man's fallen gun away. With a fluid motion, he stood, reached behind his neck and swung the knife, severing the rope just above the man's boot.

Hitting the ground, the man lay, barely conscious and groaning. Leet sretrieved his rope and began to coil it.

"Head feeling better?"

"No."

"It'll take a while. I suspect about the time you get back to town and collect your things it'll be feeling better. Especially if you're gone by the time I get there. By the way, rope isn't free."

Sitting up now, the man looked up.

"What's that mean?"

"It means you owe me for the rope. Just bought it a few towns back. Man can't just keep cutting off sections and still expect to catch cows…or varmints. I figure a new rope is about five dollars."

"I ain't gonna buy you a new rope."

Lighting quick, Leet swung a loop around the man's foot and hoisted him up.

"No, put me down. I'll pay!"

"I'm glad to see you're understanding."

⚜ ⚜ ⚜ ⚜ ⚜

Leet tied his horse and strode up the steps into Collier's bank. As usual, conversation stopped and he saw

Collier, in the back at his desk, glance up. Their eyes met. The portly man put his glasses down and came to the counter, glaring with distaste.

"We meet again, Mr. Stone."

"You paid a man's wages today?"

"Yes."

"He leave town?"

"Yes."

"You ready to leave town, Collier?"

Aghast, Collier recovered quickly.

"I have no intention of leaving town. I am the man with the money, and all others come to me with theirs."

"I see."

"I'm glad you do, Stone. You may rough up a few men, but men can be bought cheap in this territory. And I own much of this territory. Good day, Mr. Stone."

He turned his back and walked away.

Leet stood for a few moments, and then walked out.

A few minutes later, he stood brushing his horse in the livery when he heard subtle footfalls. Still brushing, his mind worked fast. When the steps settled, he shifted around the head of his horse to groom the other side. A short glance under the horse showed him three sets of boots. He slipped his hand behind his back, feeling the smooth wood handle of a pitchfork he knew was there.

"Stone, we come to persuade you to leave town."

Without responding, Leet brought the pitchfork out and under the horse's belly, slamming the tines through one of the boots. A man screamed and the moment of shock allowed another jab and another scream.

Stepping around the horse, Leet grabbed the third man and slammed his face into the corner post. The man fell and lay silent while the other two lay in the aisle clasping their feet in agony.

Pulling his pistol, Leet towered over the men and pointed the barrel at one, then the other.

"Collier?"

Neither man answered. Leet forcefully laid the barrel along one man's head, and the man crumpled. Now the gun pointed at the other man.

"You want to take a nap, too, or get a chance to see the doc? That pitchfork left a nice hole."

The man grasped his foot in agony.

"Yes! Collier sent us."

❧❧ ❧❧ ❧❧ ❧❧ ❧❧

Returning to his room, Leet lay back on the bed, thinking as he waited for the next dance in the routine.

For a man wanting to own the territory, Collier was a bit incautious. His bank was old and, even more importantly, the safe was old. The man was egotistical and confident that nobody would brace him or dare to disrupt his hold.

Leet knew every overconfident man had a weakness. During the war, it seemed the boldest, most swaggering and bragging men were the ones who ran at the first gun smoke or cowered behind a rock. It was the ones who said they were scared that seemed to find their courage.

He had a hunch about Collier. Still, the man was not

to be dismissed. Desperate men often held interesting surprises.

Hearing steps in the hall, he grasped the gun under his pillow. Sharp knocks rattled the door. Leet stood quickly.

"Come in slowly. Keep your hands where I can see them."

"Mr. Stone?"

The man was average height, prone to a bulge above the belt, with gray hair and that look of someone who is not sure of the task ahead but resigned to it. A star adorned his vest.

"Yes, Sheriff?"

The man shifted uncomfortably.

"You need to come to the jail and answer some questions."

"Not hardly."

"What?"

"Sheriff, you know as well as I do that Collier sent you, that he has you in his pocket and that your only goal in getting me to the jail is to surround me with a few guns, get mine and put me behind bars. Then you can walk around all puffed up and push your weight around. But it will never matter, because you are an absolute nobody without Collier. You gave that up somewhere along the line when you first took a few coins above your salary."

Startled and uncertain, the sheriff shifted his feet. Leet heard light footsteps on the not too distant steps.

"Stone, are you arguing with me?"

"Yep."

"I'm the sheriff."

"No you aren't. A sheriff is a man with a heart and a loyalty to the law. You are a pawn of Collier's and you are good for nothing."

"You got no call to talk like that!"

"You tell me what's not true."

Light footfalls receded down the steps.

"You need to leave town, Stone."

"I will leave when I please. On the other hand, I would suggest you, Sheriff, leave this evening."

"What?"

"You heard me."

The sheriff looked at Leet's arms and massive torso, eyes gaping.

"I…"

"I will be going to bed later, Sheriff. When I awaken in the morning, I will check and see if you are still here. If you are still in town, I will personally tie you belly-down on your horse and send you down the trail." Leet raised his pistol and pulled the hammer back. "Am I clear, Sheriff?"

ᚶᚶ ᚶᚶ ᚶᚶ ᚶᚶ ᚶᚶ

Carrie poured his coffee. The dining room was sparse, but those who were present smiled and nodded as he walked to a table. He nodded back, smiling.

Gesturing at the other tables, Carrie spoke softly.

"You've made some friends, Leet. Word gets around fast and the doctor is a talker. Collier's never liked him, but he's the only doctor for a long ways." She looked around and spoke louder. "Pitchforks make nasty holes in feet.

Doc says neither of those men will make an honest dollar for a few weeks. Says the holes went clean through and the tines weren't clean. And, by the way, the sheriff left town just a bit ago."

Leet glanced around the room. There were a few smiles and more nods his way. He spoke softly.

"What were you doing on the stairs at the hotel?"

Carrie blushed.

"How…?"

"I recognized your steps."

"Well, I…I saw Collier talking to the sheriff and then the sheriff headed to the hotel."

"What were you thinking of doing?"

"I don't know, but…" her voice firmed and she looked him in the eye. "I would have done something." She reached to her apron, where Leet could see the tug of a derringer.

"Why did you plan to help me? I'm just a stray that wandered into town."

Carrie paused, seeking the right words.

"You're…you're more of a man than most of these people have ever seen."

She blushed, but her glance did not waver.

"You mean more of a bear?"

Carrie looked at him firmly.

"No, I mean nothing of the kind. I mean man."

❧ ❧ ❧ ❧ ❧

What he did that night took care. Sleeping till midnight allowed the town to quiet. Another hour had most cowhands either headed back to the bunkhouses of their respective ranches or seeking other comforts.

Leet took his time, slipping on moccasins before he left the room. Rubbing soap on the door hinges earlier assured their silence as he slipped out. Scoping out the squeaky boards of the hallway allowed him to make as little noise as possible. Also, there were few lodgers tonight. One was a drummer peddling some sort of heal-all tonic, but had come to his room rolling drunk. Snores rattled the hall. The others were cowboys in town to blow off steam and he knew they would not be back till morning. An old drifter occupied the end room and Leet figured he'd keep to himself.

Carefully slipping by the desk where the clerk snored in a chair leaned against the wall, Leet crossed to the rear door and passed into the night.

ⴰⵝⴰ ⴰⵝⴰ ⴰⵝⴰ ⴰⵝⴰ ⴰⵝⴰ

Carrie slept fitfully, her mind cluttered.

Her life had not been what she planned, and the loss of her husband plus Collier taking the farm had been hard to take. A strong woman, she was not a quitter, but lately she wondered what the future held. Barely making ends meet as a waitress did not hold much promise. Now she had something else on her mind.

Leet Stone.

The man had come into town as a drifter, yet he was much more than that. She sensed something in him. A dream, perhaps. While so many saw him for just an incredibly big and hairy man, there was something that held her. For the first time since her husband died she found herself thinking of another man. Leet was a man both gentle and with deep strength. He did not want to fight, but did not shrink from dealing with it when it came. And he didn't toy with his opponents, but dealt with each challenge quickly and without wavering. He was well mannered and generous.

She smiled.

The town was silent as she heard something hit the window. She waited a moment, listening. It happened again. Arising, she grabbed her wrap and slipped it on as she went to the window.

Looking down, she saw a large form standing below.

Awareness dawned and she raised the sash.

Leet gestured to be quiet. His face was only slightly illumined as clouds drifted across the moon. He gestured to the door of the kitchen below.

Descending the steps, she unlatched the door. Leet took a quick look around and slipped into the room. He carried a bundle.

"Are we alone?"

"Yes." She nervously clasped her wrap tighter.

He smiled kindly.

"Carrie, I'd never do that. I need your help with something. Pull all the curtains."

It took but a moment to draw the curtains securely. Leet looked around, then lit a small lamp on the table.

"What is this all about, Leet?"

Handing her a ledger, he pointed to it.

"Recognize the names in there?"

Turning the cover, her mouth opened wide. Startled, she looked up at Leet.

"This is Collier's bank ledger! How…?"

"Ever hear the story of Robin Hood? Take from the rich and give to the poor?"

"Yes, but…Leet, what is this all about."

"It's about…this."

He opened the bundle and dumped a pile of cash and papers on the table, along with a bag of coins.

"Leet, did you…did you rob Collier's bank?"

"Carrie, you need to understand something."

"You robbed the bank?"

"No, I merely removed Collier's ill-gotten gains. It's time to return them to where they belong." He pointed to the ledger. "I need your help to sort this out."

Carrie stared…then slowly broke into a smile.

"How did you get this?"

"Collier has an old safe. I watched him this afternoon. He carries a key around his neck, but he kept touching the blotting pad on his desk. I guessed and, sure enough, he had another key under the corner. The ledger was in his desk drawer. All the papers were sitting in the safe."

An hour later, they sat back, piles separated and placed into envelopes with cash totals and deeds and promissory notes.

Leet waited downstairs while Carrie changed clothes and returned.

"We don't have long…maybe an hour, before I need

to get the stoves going. The good thing is I'm running the restaurant alone this morning."

൦൦ൟ ൦൦ൟ ൦൦ൟ ൦൦ൟ ൦൦ൟ

There were shocked looks all over town that morning, as people opened doors to do their chores and found envelopes tucked into the jambs. There was cash equaling their payments, along with all notes of obligation to Collier. It didn't take long for most to sense something miraculous in the wind. Most burned the papers without delay.

The dining room was full that morning, and Carrie was both extra tired and busy. Still, her smile was winsome and did not flag when Collier walked in.

Collier stared, irritated, as his designated table was occupied.

Carrie looked over and smiled sweetly.

"Have a table for you soon, Mr. Collier."

Collier spoke in a demanding tone.

"Why is my table taken?"

"Busy this morning. Goodness, going through eggs this morning! Might not have any by the time you get seated."

Collier frowned and, glancing around, spotted Leet sitting at a prominent table in the corner, smiling and talking with an elderly lady. They laughed. Then Leet met Collier's eyes and smiled, lifting his cup and nodding.

"Good morning, Mr. Collier."

"What's so good about it?"

"People are talking all over town. Robin Hood came

last night."

"Robin Hood? Are you daft? Besides, I thought the sheriff told you to leave town?" Nodding to his guard, he hissed, "Get the sheriff."

Leet settled into his eggs and steak, savoring the taste and enjoying the happiness settling on the town.

A few minutes later, Collier's guard returned.

"Well, where's the sheriff?"

"He's gone, Mr. Collier? Word is he left yesterday."

"Well, find him!"

"No…I mean, he's gone. Gone. Left town. His horse is gone and his blankets and saddlebags are gone."

Collier glanced at Leet.

"Why is everybody eating here today? They've got payments to make."

Leet smiled at Carrie. Grinning, she filled another cup for the mercantile owner.

"Thank you, Carrie."

A man rushed into the room, looked to Collier and spoke hurriedly.

"Mr. Collier! The bank. Back door was open."

Collier rushed from the room.

Leet looked around the room, then to Carrie.

"I'm going to step outside."

"Be careful, Leet. Please. I don't want you hurt."

His smile lingered an extra moment. Stepping out the door, he walked slowly to the street. There he leaned against a post, waiting.

Collier strode back ten minutes later. Anger flushed his face.

Stopping a few yards from Leet, he yelled:

"You robbed the bank! You robbed my bank! That is my money these people are so happily spending!"

"That's a strong accusation. Do you have any witnesses?"

"I don't need any witnesses! Everybody knows it was you!"

"Do you have any proof these people owe you money?"

Collier stared, then calmed strangely.

"I'll take care of you, Stone. Then, I'll get my men and we'll go house to house and take it back."

"I don't like bankers like you, Collier. Sort of goes way back. I suggest you get on your horse and leave."

Collier glared, then looked over Leet's left shoulder. Just the briefest flicker. Then he turned away.

Leet saw it. He knew it from experience. The sudden calming, the glance, the way Collier held his wrist.

Sure enough. Leet caught the reflection in the shop window across the street as a rifle came over the false front of the building behind him.

Turning, he drew and stepped to the side as he shot. Without waiting, he turned back to see Collier grinning with his gun coming out of his waist and straightening. Leet fired and Collier stumbled backwards, grasping at his chest. He fell to the ground. Spinning again, Leet looked back to the roof to see Collier's guard hanging lifeless over the false front.

Carrie rushed from the restaurant to his side.

An hour later he had his horse saddled and hitched to the post in front of the restaurant.

Carrie stood with him. Sadness filled her eyes.

"Leet…?"

"I can't see anything here for me now, Carrie."

Tears welled in her eyes.

"Leet, I…well, I'm here."

"There's no place for me here. The people, like everywhere else I've been, just want me to leave. It's been the pattern over the years."

At that moment, an elderly lady approached, followed by a gathering group of townsfolk. She gently urged Carrie to the side and looked into Leet's eyes.

"Mr. Stone?"

"Yes, ma'am."

Pointing to the gathering crowd, she spoke with a smile.

"You made a difference to all of us. Collier was a crook and stole from us. You didn't need to return our money. You could have taken off in the night. But you didn't. You cared for us." She glanced at Carrie. "And I think you care for Carrie here. A lot. I ain't no spring chicken but I can see she cares for you, too."

"Ma'am…"

"Now hush, Mr. Stone. Here's what I got to say." She looked to the crowd. "We had a talk amongst us and we want you to stay."

"Well, ma'am…"

"Don't 'well, ma'am' me, Mr. Stone. We've got a strong need for a man like you in a very important job."

"What job, ma'am?"

She looked around to the crowd and one by one they

came forward and held out envelopes. Leet recognized the envelopes.

"We need a banker, Mr. Stone. One we can trust."

Leet was stunned. All around him were nods and out-thrust envelopes. He looked to Carrie. Yearning showed in her eyes. He paused for a very long moment.

"I'm sorry, all of you. I cannot take those envelopes today."

Disappointed sighs filled the air.

"Mr. Stone…" It was the elderly lady again.

Leet held up his hand, silencing the crowd.

"I can't take those envelopes today. Today is my wedding day…I think."

He looked to Carrie and held out his hand. Wiping her tears, she snuggled next to him and spoke softly.

"It's a grand day for a wedding, Leet."

The crowd cheered.

"We'll need a honeymoon. Have to be in a big town."

"Why?"

"Have to buy a better safe!"

BEECHER'S FOLLY

Half blind and stiff with age, the yellow dog slowly climbed the steps as Zion Beecher exited the bank and, seeing the dog, reared his foot back for a kick.

"Get out of my way, you old cur!"

The kick was never completed, for into the silence came the sound of a cold voice from the back of a horse at the hitch rail.

"I wouldn't do that if I was you."

Looking belligerent, Zion hesitated. The dog waddled out of his way.

Zion Beecher was a big man, both in stature and community standing. He was accustomed to people stepping aside for him and nodding in deferential respect. That he was rude and the respect was grudging made no difference to him. Nobody challenged Zion Beecher.

Except at home. There, Irene Beecher was undisputed queen of the house. Outside the house, Zion Beecher held sway, but the moment he entered the house, he was in another kingdom. Irene was no pushover, and when he married her – for her dowry – she laid down the law. That first night he slapped her and she glared at him as she felt her face. Not another word was said. In the night he awoke to find her gone and located her in the kitchen, a pot of water boiling on the stove.

"What's that for?" he asked gruffly.

"That's to pour on you while you're asleep."

He never struck her again and, though he blustered and strutted elsewhere, at home they settled into a comfortable and respectful existence. Irene Beecher liked the trappings of wealth and the deferential looks of those around. Zion Beecher made sure she had what she wanted. And they held immense parties to parade their power.

He was the undisputed lord of the kingdom…except the house.

He grew up one of many children begotten by a street tough. Struggling to survive and subject to frequent beatings by about anybody, he finally started to beat up on those smaller than himself. Eventually, he found it was easier to pay others to do the beatings for him. He saved his hands to handle money he extorted and stole from others. Then one night he managed to break into the safe of his rival. Giving his pursuers the slip, he carried many thousands in cash and took a train headed the best direction – away – and learned the cattle trade. For fifteen years now he'd lived like a lord. But he wanted more, and the spreads around held enough cattle to double his holdings and make him a man wealthy for life.

Before him now sat this stranger, clothes and face gray with the dust of a long trail. A once-brown hat was stained and sagged from the ravages of weather. Looking like many other saddle tramps, something about the gun at his hip said he was different. Hard trails were etched in his face and punctuated by the set of his mouth. But it was the eyes that arrested Zion. It was as if he stared into the eyes of the Grim Reaper himself and it seemed a cold wind caused him to shiver in the oppressive summer heat. The horse the stranger rode had the appearance of barely restrained wildness.

Beecher, long able to sense fear and quickly take advantage of it, saw no fear in this man. The stranger was immovable and uncowed. It was as if he, Zion, meant absolutely nothing to him. That should have been enough to bring on outrage but, instead, something within Zion Beecher felt the sting of fear.

Beecher gained his composure and held his head high. Red-faced, a glance to the side showed him a couple of bystanders and he knew what happened now would be told around town within minutes.

"Do you know who I am?"

"Don't care." The voice was cold.

"I'm Zion Beecher. I own the Lazy-Z and half the country around." He looked to the gathering crowd with pleasure, for most of these people were peons in his realm and dependent upon him in some way for their meager livelihood.

"It takes a big man to kick an old dog. I'm almighty impressed."

A white-haired Mexican, leaning against a post nearby, chuckled.

Beecher, red-faced, glanced over. The small man showed no emotion.

A clatter of running horses brought a smirk of satisfaction and victory to Beecher. The horses stopped and the leader stepped down and strode to Beecher's side. He was a man with a twice-broken nose and a glint of evil delight in his eye.

"A problem, Mr. Beecher?" His attitude was cocky as he glanced at the stranger and then to the Mexican.

"Wilkins, that Mex is being uppity. And this here – drifter – needs to know who's boss in these parts."

Wilkins stared at the stranger on the horse. His gut turned cold and he immediately sensed this man was pure poison. As one timber wolf meets another, Wilkins felt the challenge. He turned to the Mexican.

"Mex, I ain't seen you before. Where'd you come from?"

"My mother, señor."

"Your mother? Why, you…" About to go after the man, he heard the stranger speak in a voice edged with steel.

"Wouldn't do that if I was you."

Wilkins, wary but puffed up with his own importance and the handful of men fanning out around the stranger, spoke with bluster. "Mister, I got men all around you. The cards you hold are a losing hand. I think you need to get down and apologize to Mr. Beecher."

"Ain't gonna happen."

Wilkins glanced to his men. "It ain't a request."

A voice came from one of the men.

"Boss, that there is Liam Henry."

Wilkins paused, eyes narrowed. Liam Henry! Known as one of the fastest and deadliest gunmen ever to ride the

West. With a draw said to match the flash of lightning, it was rumored even the name brought sweat to the brows of known gunfighters like Bill Longley and others. Liam Henry was a loner riding the West and seeming to have no direction other than the way his horse was pointed.

Grinning, Wilkins looked to the dust and spit. "Liam Henry, gunman." The glint brightened in his eye. "I would love to have your notch on my gun!"

"Try any time. Been others who had the same hankering."

"Well, there's no way you'll leave here alive, Henry. You got guns all around you."

"I won't die alone. First the fat man, then you. By then I might catch some lead, but with the horses starting to jump, who knows. Might even get a third before I go down. Go ahead and make your play. I just don't care."

Zion Beecher, incensed but grasping truth, interrupted sourly. "Wilkins, we're on a schedule. Kill him later."

Wilkins smiled. "Till next time, Henry. Hope it's not too long." He looked at the Mexican. "We'll deal with you later."

After the riders moved off, Liam looked to the Mexican.

"Pacheco. It's good to see you, my friend."

"Señor Liam, it has been a while. From the look on your face, life has been hard."

"It's a hard life."

"That it is, señor."

Two years earlier, they met on the trail and spent a few miles together. Something in the loneliness of each of their lives found a brief respite in those miles. Liam Henry was a man of few words, but Pacheco was one of the few who could draw him out. It was easy company and when they parted, each knew the other was a friend.

Standing in the livery stable later, they tightened the cinches on their horses.

"I think Wilkins will follow you."

"Likely will, Pacheco. His kind has a lust to prove something. His manhood will not allow him to let me go untried."

"And so it continues – and you will have to move on again, señor."

"It always happens that way. And you?"

"He will seek me out to show how he can treat a Mexican."

"Likely."

"Do you ever wonder about going somewhere far away, señor?"

"To get away from my reputation? Change names?"

"Si."

"I tried that. Went to St. Louis. Lots of people. Walking down the street one day I ran into someone that knew me from Tombstone and had convinced himself he had something to prove. Few men, once they have a reputation, ever get a chance to rest. And I can't stand the crowds in a city. It's the wide open spaces that draw me, Pacheco."

Pacheco nodded. "Where are you headed from here?"

"About thirty miles north. A friend has a ranch. Losing cows to rustlers."

Pacheco nodded again. "So you go to meet trouble."

"Yes."

"It is something that needs to be done. So much of life is that way. We think we make choices, but then it might appear our choice is laid aside and we do what must be done. Such as now. I have a choice as well...but do I, really?" He grinned. "You say you travel north?"

"Yes."

"North is a good direction. Do you think your friend would mind if you were not alone?"

Liam Henry turned. "It's your choice, friend. I can speak for you." He chuckled. "Might be necessary, in fact. You don't really look like much."

Pacheco nodded and smiled.

Hovering at five-foot, Pacheco weighed a mite over a hundred pounds soaking wet. White haired at an early age, wrinkled from the decades and squinting into the sun, his age was but a guess. After weeks in the mountains, he finally came to this town, found a mirror and shaved. His bedroll was in the loft of the livery as usual, as no hotel was willing to let a room to him. Quiet and preferring anonymity, he was often mistaken as weak. Pacheco was far from that - strength lay just below the surface. Though he visibly carried only a rifle, his skill with a knife was unrivaled.

Pacheco was a man of deep faith, crossing himself before meals, before he started his day and, when possible, before defending himself. His pockets were near empty most of the time, for he had a habit of slipping coins to those in need.

Riding out of the livery, Liam headed towards the

saloon.

"Let's stop for a drink before we ride out."

"Señor, I am not welcome in the saloon."

"You're with me."

Pacheco shrugged and followed.

Entering the saloon and pausing to let his eyes adjust, Liam watched as heads turned and measured glances flicked over and turned behind him to linger on Pacheco. Eyes narrowed. A couple of town folk left quietly, knowing trouble was at hand.

Liam walked to the bar and glanced in the mirror. The few tables were partly filled with men. He knew it was the wrong time of day for cowhands to gather, and the dress of most showed these were no thirty-a-month hands. These men were hired for other reasons.

Liam slapped coins on the bar. "Whiskey. The same for my friend."

Setting a single glass on the bar before Liam, the man poured a drink. Liam coldly looked at the man, who visibly faltered as the icy voice spoke. "I said one for my friend."

Voice cracking, the bartender said, "Don't serve his kind here," glancing at Pacheco.

Liam's hand grabbed the man's shirt collar and dragged him half over the bar. Chairs were heard to push away from tables as Liam pulled the man to within an inch of his face and fairly hissed, "This hombre is my friend, and you will serve him a drink. Is that understood?"

Choking, the man's eyes were bulging.

"Yes," he choked.

Liam shoved him backwards. The bartender recovered, set another glass and poured. His hand shook and a full measure hit the bar before the glass was filled. Pacheco took the glass and quietly said, "Gracias."

Glancing in the mirror and seeing two men standing, Liam turned. His hand hovered meaningfully at hip level. One man wore a black and white spotted cowhide vest, the other a green shirt with gold braid on the pockets.

"You gents got a problem?"

"Mister, you and your friend need to leave."

Pacheco quietly faced the bar.

One man's eyes narrowed with thought.

"Bart, I don't think…"

The man with the gold braid reached for his gun. In the blink of an eye he lay dead, red mixing with the green and gold. Liam's gun covered the other man, who stood immobile and staring into the fire of Liam Henry's eyes.

"What's your decision?"

"I ain't drawing."

Liam hissed out the words: "Then sit down!"

The man carefully sat.

Nobody moved, seeing the look in Liam's eyes. A mere flicker of movement would result in more death and they knew it. A fly walked across one man's nose and it took all he had to suppress the need to swat at it.

Finally, Liam holstered his gun and turned back to the bar. There was an audible sigh of relief throughout the room.

Minutes later the batwings swung open and the sheriff entered. He paused and surveyed the room, taking in the body on the floor and the feeling the tension. Someone nodded towards Liam and the sheriff turned to the bar. Standing to one side, he was wary as he spoke.

"You kill this man?"

"He drew first."

The sheriff shifted uneasily.

The man with the spotted vest spoke with a touch of nervousness.

"Sheriff, we all saw it. Gunderson drew first."

Looking hard at Liam, he read the moment and nodded.

"Ok, fair fight. A couple of you men drag the body out of here. You," he pointed to Liam and Pacheco, "It's better you get on your horses and go. Beecher'll be madder than a wet hen. He won't push it in town, but I carry no weight when you ride out."

"Sheriff, I don't care what the fat man thinks. But it just so happens we had no intention of staying. All we wanted was a quick drink and then to ride on. Your bartender was rude and green shirt fancied himself a fast draw. I hope nobody else makes any mistakes." He scanned the room. "But have at it if you will."

๑๑๑ ๑๑๑ ๑๑๑ ๑๑๑ ๑๑๑

"My friend, you will be proud of me."

"Why's that?" Liam asked.

"Because I really have stayed away from trouble for six months now."

Liam chuckled. It was a rare sound in his life. Somehow this simple Mexican man was able to reach a different part of his soul. It was a welcome interlude in the life of a loner always on the edge of violence and pursuit. Though he tried to stay on the right side of the law, it wasn't always the case and he straddled the fence many a time. It was a lonely life. Still, when a man was alone, he was often safer. When confronted, he could shoot without wondering if the target was a friend.

"My Mexican friend, have you ever thought of stopping, putting down roots and finding a woman?"

"It crosses my mind once in a while, especially in the cold of winter when I shiver in my blankets for many days on end. It would be a comfort. The Bible says, 'Where two lie down together there is warmth.' But with that warmth comes trouble also. Before you know it, a woman would make me take my shoes off in the house, and I would have to be home for dinner. And if she saw me look too long at another señorita…well…sleeping in the barn is worse than outside! That kind of life has never seemed to fit for me. Still, there was a young lady once who turned my eye."

"What was her name?"

"Valencia."

"Pretty name. Ever wonder about her?"

"I think of her now and then on the lonely trails. But she is married now – to my friend Carlos. They are happy. I have seen them. Carlos is happy with his house and seeks to please Valencia. But it is not a life for me."

"Me, neither."

"Have you ever dreamed of a special woman, Liam?"

"Never was much of a hand with decent women. Can you imagine if we had a woman here? The camp would have to be set up as she pleased and probably have to carry plates and teacups!"

Both men laughed.

"Still," Liam said, "When the gray hair comes, the trails may be lonelier and the ground harder. Might be pleasant to have walls and a roof and a decent meal."

"Si."

⚜ ⚜ ⚜ ⚜ ⚜

Early the next day they topped a ridge overlooking a small but beautiful valley. A stream ran through the middle and a cabin nestled in the far corner on the highest point. The view from the cabin would take in the most likely approaches.

"It is beautiful, señor."

"Ralston Conner. Goes by Rally. We went through a scrape together down to New Mexico a few years back. He took a bullet that lodged in his back. Gives him some trouble. But he had this dream and saw this valley a couple years before and pegged it as the place he wanted. When he was able to get out of bed, he waved goodbye to the wandering life and settled here. I came by once last year. He was doing well. Went to the breaks in the mountains and found a lot of mavericks, fetched himself a wife and built his dream. Nigh on to five hundred head when I was here. Stacey makes a mean beef stew."

Liam reined to a stop, looking across the valley.

"What is it, señor?"

"Something is not right, Pacheco. Where are the cattle?"

❧❧ ❧❧ ❧❧ ❧❧ ❧❧

The house door hung open, creaking as it moved in the breeze. Corral bars lay where they were pulled apart. What had happened?

As Liam approached, he spotted a man in the shadows of the porch. The man arose from the chair he had propped again the wall. Squinting, it was clear he had been dozing.

"Hold it right there, mister."

Liam rode a couple paces further before stopping. The man walked into the sun.

"This ain't no place for a drifter. Might as well just turn your horse away and ride."

"This is the Conner place. Where's Rally and his wife?"

"This place is abandoned. Beecher's gonna file on it."

"Rally Conner would never leave this place. What happened?"

Lifting his rifle, the man gestured.

"Mister, I told you to leave."

At that moment Pacheco, slipping around the corner, cocked his rifle.

"Any move whatsoever will make you a dead man, señor."

Disarming the guard, Liam spoke firmly, "Where Are Rally and Stacey?"

"I don't know nothin' about the folks that used to live here. I just hired on and was told to guard the place."

"Guard against what?"

Hesitating, the man jerked as Liam backhanded him across the mouth. Blood began to seep.

"I asked you a question." Liam raised his hand again.

"No! It ain't no never mind to me. Wilkins said there was a woman out here and we was to keep her from the house."

Pacheco had been looking around the valley. Now he pointed.

"Señor?"

Over against the trees in the distance were two mounds. Old dried flowers lay scattered on both.

"Who's buried yonder?"

"One is Conner. I don't know about the other."

Tying the guard, they mounted and rode over, eyes scanning all directions.

"Liam, I think a child is also buried here."

"Hair on my neck is up, Pacheco. I feel eyes on us."

"I feel the same way, señor."

They dismounted and stood between their horses, scanning the hills, hats pulled low against the glare.

Liam's eyes paused at a deep stand of brush.

"Someone there, off to the right of that clump."

"I see it."

A voice hailed.

"Liam Henry?"

Liam frowned and called back. "Stacey?"

A woman in a torn and dirty dress emerged from the brush. Still young, the mark of hard living was upon her, with sun-browned skin and early wrinkles. Her feet were clad in moccasins and her hair lacked proper care. But the Winchester in her hands was well kept. She walked towards them, the step of a tired person.

"Liam. I knew you'd come. Rally said I could count on it."

He held out his arms and she dropped the gun to her side and leaned against him and sobbed.

"What happened, Stacey?"

"It was Zion Beecher's men. They started thinning our herd about seven months ago. Zion came by and told us he wanted this valley and he gave us a week to get out. You know Rally – he told Beecher where he could put his notion. We knew there'd be trouble and started keeping a rifle in that hollow tree there, along with a pack to grab quick. But Rally's back was gettin' troublesome – he took spells of that – and he could hardly stand at times. About a week ago, Beecher's man Wilkins came over with a handful of others and called Rally out." Stacey paused, tears forming and running down her cheeks. "It was a real bad day for his back and Wilkins laughed at him. Told him how Beecher'd have the land and he'd have me. He looked at me in a terrible way. Rally drew on him and Wilkins shot him. He's fast, Liam. Mighty fast. I turned to run to the brush. A couple men tried to catch me and I winged one with my derringer. They stopped and hollered they would get me later. I saw them head to the house and heard them tearing things apart. Well, I seen Rally was dead, so I grabbed the gun and pack and headed to the hills. I watched from the woods when they tied a rope to Rally's feet and had a horse haul him over here. Didn't do a good job. They left a guard that night but I watched and he found our whiskey and got drunk and passed out. I came back and fetched some food and covered Rally better. The man started to stir and

I laid him out cold. The next day they came back and tried to find me, but I kept moving. Been a man here ever since, sometimes two. I haven't been able to get into the house again."

Rally glanced to the mounds.

"There's two graves."

Stacey's head dropped.

"I was with child. Rally was so excited. But the second day after they were chasing me, I was plumb wore out and fell. Landed bad and lost the baby. Baby Gabe. Gabriel Conner. I buried him at night also."

⚜ ⚜ ⚜ ⚜ ⚜

Walking into the cabin, Liam and Pacheco saw the mess of the guards and the evidence of their looting. About to turn and walk out, Liam spotted the cradle sitting in a corner. A tobacco stain was strewn across the side. Anger rose in his heart. He went to the barn at dusk and saddled the guard's horse. Throwing the man face down over the saddle, hands tied underneath, Liam spoke to the man.

"You tell Beecher I'm coming for him. There is no place to hide." He slapped the horse.

"Señor, I give it a mile and he will slip underneath the horse and have a mighty uncomfortable ride."

"He deserves worse."

Pacheco stared at the house a moment.

"She will need time, señor. I think she needs a bath. I will let you get the water. I will see about finding some rabbits for supper."

A couple hours passed with Stacey by herself in the cabin. Liam could hear her straightening the mess, then he filled buckets for her and she bathed while he chopped some wood. He paused frequently to scan the trail and the hills. Though he didn't expect anything tonight, it was never bad to be cautious.

ᏬᎧ ᏬᎧ ᏬᎧ ᏬᎧ ᏬᎧ

That evening, they sat quietly at the table, picking at their food. Pacheco had scared up a couple rabbits and the aroma filled the room but could not cut through the somber mood. Stacey was exhausted. She wore a colorful calico dress that somehow survived the looting. Her hair was knotted atop her head. But she was quiet and leaned upon her hand, struggling to stay awake.

Liam's mind worked through ideas. After hearing Stacey out, he knew something must be done. But not a personal vendetta. That could come later. The best way to hurt Zion Beecher was in the wallet.

He glanced over at his friend's widow. Tired and suffering through the loss of both husband and child, she had the strength to hide out in the hills and hang on. She definitely had backbone. Her eyes were half shut with sleep when she turned to Pacheco and Liam in turn.

"We had a lot of dreams for this place. Rally knew his strength was failing at times, but he had determination – grit. The days he had his strength he worked hard. The other days he planned." Moisture filled her eyes. "I loved him." She paused. "But Rally reminded me when the trouble started, no matter what, I was to move forward. Always forward he said. Don't look back. Well, now he's gone and I must go forward."

"Stacey, you need to get to bed. We'll watch."

She nodded and slowly went to the bed in a little alcove and lay down, pulling the coverlet over herself. It seemed like mere seconds and they heard soft breathing.

"Señor? Do you think Beecher has run those cows to market yet, or is he holding them in a convenient spot?"

"Just wondering the same thing. Might be he's holding them, plus others, until he gains possession of the spreads. Then nobody'd question the ownership of the cattle. Might be best to go check. Beecher's been working to get more territory. Could be he's got his hands gathering and driving in the other directions. I know a valley not too far from here, and it's a place he could use to hold a large herd and have just a man or two on watch. I think maybe we check it out. We'll leave in the morning."

"I'm going along." It was Stacey.

"Thought you was asleep."

She stared, "Habits don't change so quick."

"Only got two horses."

Stacey looked at him. "Sure to be an extra or so at the herd. Probably our horses anyhow. It wouldn't be stealing if I took them back."

Liam nodded.

❦ ❦ ❦ ❦ ❦

Early that morning, before they rode out, Stacey went

into the house and pried up a board in the floor. Underneath was a small bundle, which she unwrapped. A poke jingled with coins. Next to it was a folded sheet of paper that she placed into her pocket.

She walked out into the sunlight and glanced around. The porch was filthy, and she'd have to sweep it when they returned. It was hard to picture the ranch without Rally, but it was still home.

Liam rode with Stacey behind his saddle. Conversation flowed, with Stacey eager to talk. Finally, reaching the notch where the hills flowed into the northern valley, they reined up and Stacey slid off. Peering through the trees for a few minutes, she looked back. Liam and Pacheco dismounted.

"Near six hundred head or so, rough count. So it's more than mine. Lots of young stock."

Pacheco smiled. "I see a campsite over near that outcropping. I see one bedroll. Beecher's pretty confident."

Liam nodded.

"My guess is that cowhand ain't the brightest in Beecher's stable. Good chance he's been here a while and don't know nothin' about what happened in town."

"What are you thinking, señor?"

"I think I work for Beecher."

Stacey's eyes widened with a question. Liam looked to them both.

"You two wait here. Stay out of sight."

He rode down the hillside, whistling.

Stacey looked at Pacheco.

"Rally said it was always best to be on Liam's side in a

fight. Told me Liam was deadly when he got real riled up. I wonder, Pacheco, what made him that way?"

"The ways of a man are hard to figure, Stacey. I do not know much about Liam other than he carries something – deep within – that keeps him restless and barely contains the embers of a fire. It is a fire that takes very little breeze to bring it to a flame. When it does flare up, it is not good. I do not know, but I think that somewhere back down a trail long ago, something happened that he cannot let go of."

ᘉ ᘉ ᘉ ᘉ ᘉ

Sitting his horse, the cowhand watched as Liam neared. He was young, probably all of sixteen. Liam noted his inexperience by the thong still over the hammer of his pistol.

Beecher was certainly confident in the safety of this herd.

"Howdy, Gantner."

"I'm Smith. Who's Gantner?"

"I'm mixed up. He did say Smith was with the herd. Gantner's waiting for us over to Graysville."

"Gantner? Never heard of him. And waiting for who?"

"Us…and the herd. Gantner is a buyer. Beecher wants us to move the herd towards Graysville."

"I ain't heard from nobody. And who are you?"

"Liam Hanks. Wilkins hired me couple days back to round up strays. Said he had a good man watching the herd and I was to go help him."

Smith puffed up with pride. Still, there was suspicion.

"But Wilkins was here last week. Said they would move in about two weeks. Brought me grub and said wouldn't be anybody here before then and I was to sit tight."

"Beecher changed his mind, I guess."

"What for?"

"Didn't ask. Something was going on. The conversation was a bit hot and they shut up when I come by. Beecher looked awful mean in the eyes and I figured it wasn't time to ask questions."

Smith softened a mite. "I guess Beecher can make up his own mind. He does have a powerful temper. I just say, 'yes, sir' and do what he says. That there Wilkins is a mite eager to quarrel, if you know what I mean."

"Yes, seems like his trigger finger was a bit itchy, and that Colt of his was slung pretty loose."

Liam's familiarity with Beecher and Wilkins set the boy at ease.

Glancing to the cattle nearby, Liam noted several with Rally's brand. But most of the others were unbranded young animals less than a year old. These were undoubtedly the young calves of the area herds. Any unbranded cattle found on the range would by custom be branded with a running brand or cinch ring. Cowboys were not always too particular about the mother's brand. Many a herd in the West was built that way and some great cattlemen began with questionable methods. In these times, the running brand was still used, but frowned upon and open to question.

"Lot's of young, unbranded calves, Smith. Maybe Beecher planned to do a road brand."

"I dunno. This is my first herd job. Just supposed to watch over them until I get word. Usually Wilkins comes by. I do recall him saying they would brand later. The men were occupied with other jobs. They brought in a couple hundred head last week."

Liam chuckled to himself. Sure they were busy with other jobs. Stealing cattle. Hazing off only the young, unbranded animals. Lot's of them this time of year before branding.

"Well, I figure we better move them a bit to the north. Might make a few miles by nightfall. Why don't you go pack up your camp while I get them started."

While they moved the herd, Liam casually grouped a few young, unbranded cows. Waving Smith to go ahead to the point, Liam took the opportunity to head the unbranded to a meadow behind the hillside. With only a half dozen horses, he was hesitant to separate one but knew it was a risk he had to take.

That night he told Smith he was going to take a ride around the herd. He rode back and knew he'd find Pacheco and Stacey following. They were in a clump of trees and a tiny fire signaled their location. It would be visible only at certain points he would have to ride when looking for them. Hailing, he sat down for a cup of coffee.

"Pacheco, you had much experience with a cinch ring?"

"Enough, señor."

"Well, I've bunched a few head into a meadow up ahead. Young, no brand. A horse, too. Need the R-C on all of them."

Pacheco smiled.

ⷮⷮ ⷮⷮ ⷮⷮ ⷮⷮ ⷮⷮ

A week later, Smith rode alongside Liam. He was silent for a while. Liam had noticed him looking over the herd. Finally, Smith got up the courage to speak.

"Seems like I'm seeing some fresh brands. R-C brands."

"Yep." He looked to the young man. "Smith. I'm going to ask you a straight question and I want a straight answer. How you answer will tell what happens next." He fixed Smith with a stare. "Are you an honest man?"

"Well…yes. For the most part."

"If I told you a lot of these cattle were stolen from a man and a woman and the man killed, would that bother you?"

"I don't hold with killin' nor botherin' women."

"Well, Smith, Beecher stole the R-C cattle and killed my friend and ran his wife into the hills trying to kill her. She got away but lost her baby. In my book that's two murders. I been figuring on getting' what's owed her and I been pushing a few cows off the trail. The widow woman and a friend of mine have been branding on the off days and driving them in the night to catch up. When we get to Graysville, Beecher will be fit to be tied."

Smith stared at him, then smiled. "I wondered why we was running slow. Daggone. An' you say Beecher killed her man and tried to kill her."

"Yep. So…where do you stand?"

"I reckon I stand with the lady. Might be a bit of trouble if'n Wilkins catches wind, though."

"He will, and there will be trouble. You just let me handle it."

"Liam? What about cows that been stolen from other ranchers?"

"We'll note the obvious brands and settle up later. But the bulk will be ours, since we don't know who lost what and how many. They likely don't either. The other ranchers will understand and be glad the rustling is stopped."

ठाठ ठाठ ठाठ ठाठ ठाठ

"Jackson, I left instructions for Smith to hold them here." Wilkins was angry and staring across the valley.

Jackson was walking his horse around glancing at the ground.

"Another rider came in here, Boss. Looks like whoever it was had a talk with Smith." He took off his hat and slapped the dust off. "Looks like the cattle been moved north."

"How long ago?"

"Probably a week."

"Who knows how far they'd be if'n we hadn't come by!"

"They's a piece down the trail."

"Jackson, you go get Bannon and Trotsky at the line shack. Probably Kelly, too. Get them and angle north to meet me. Send Kelly to tell Beecher. I'll follow and hang back till you get here. I think we all know who is behind this – Liam Henry and that Mex."

"What are you planning to do when we find them?"

"Kill them."

⚛ ⚛ ⚛ ⚛ ⚛

Stacey rode behind the herd with Liam.

"You keep lookin' back, Liam?"

"I got this feeling we're being followed. This has worked too smooth."

"Seen anything?"

"No."

"Tomorrow afternoon we should reach Graysville."

"Something will either happen before then or in town, Stacey. Depends on how close they are."

Pacheco and Smith rode back.

"They come, señor. I feel it."

"I feel it, too, Pacheco."

Pacheco looked behind, then to the north, where the herd was headed. "I wonder, señor, if it might be best to drive the herd through the night. Might lose a few, but that is not our biggest worry."

"You're probably right, Pacheco." He looked around. "Let's stop over by those rocks and have some coffee. Better make it strong. Gonna be a long night."

⚛ ⚛ ⚛ ⚛ ⚛

Zion Beecher was seething. To have the herd stolen from him was an affront he could not tolerate. Now he was riding towards Graysville with murder on his mind. He'd done away with Rally Conner a week ago and none of the others ranchers showed any sign of fighting back. His initial explanations of what might happen to their wives and children had been effective.

Everything had gone as planned, until Liam Henry stuck his nose in where it didn't belong. When his man rode in a few days back, about half dead from riding under his horse's belly, Zion knew action was needed. Well, it was time to take care of this once and for all.

Bringing three men, he rode with determination.

⚜ ⚜ ⚜ ⚜ ⚜

Liam and Stacey rode into Graysville mid-morning, trail-weary and covered with dust. Townsfolk put aside their chores and stood on the boardwalk as cattle milled and bellowed in the distance. They rode to the saloon, tied their horses and stretched their legs. It wasn't long before two men came through the batwings into the sunlight. One had a fine cigar and took it out of his mouth before speaking.

"Heard you coming an hour ago."

Liam looked at the man.

"You buyers?"

"Yep, if it's a legitimate herd."

"It is. Rally Conner. R-C spread, south of here. But I will lay all the cards on the table, gents. Rustler's had the herd and we took it back. You'll see other brands in the mix, but we plan to keep a tally and give them their due.

But there's a lot of young, unbranded cows. Rustlers separated them, and they can't be returned, so we'll claim them as our wages. But trouble will be here soon. Some mighty unhappy fellows behind us."

"You Rally?"

"Nope. Rally was murdered. This is his wife, Stacey Conner."

The men took off their hats.

"Sorry to hear, ma'am. We'll send some men out to make a tally. Bet you could use a good meal. Best place is the rooming house yonder." He pointed. "Probably got a place where you can freshen up. The meal is on me."

At that moment there was a pounding of horse hooves in the dust and Wilkins and the others rode up. It was clear their horses were tired and Wilkins was in a foul mood.

"Henry!" His eyes flashed to Liam and flamed. Moving to Stacey, he frowned. Then he spoke to the few on the boardwalk.

"These are rustler's! Took Beecher's herd. Where's the sheriff?"

"I'm the sheriff." a man walked through the gathering crowd.

Wilkins dismounted and strutted up the walk. "Sheriff, I demand these two be arrested for rustling!"

"Mister, you can't demand anything here." The sheriff turned to Stacey and tipped his hat. "Ma'am, you got any proof of the brand?"

Wilkins smiled, but his smile quickly faded as Stacey reached into an inner pocket of her skirt and produced a worn document.

"I believe this is what you gentlemen need to see?" She glanced at Liam. "Rally said I might need this someday."

Liam watched Wilkins closely.

The sheriff glanced at the document. "Brand registration. R-C, belongs to Rally Conner and his wife, Stacey. Looks like proof to me, gentlemen."

Wilkins blustered, "But most of them is unbranded calves!"

Liam turned to face Wilkins. "The question I have is how do you know that? And I think a good look will tell you many of them carry the R-C brand."

"Why, you…" Wilkins went for his gun.

Liam Henry expected it and was ready. He cleared leather before Wilkins and saw his expression as the bullet tore into him. Wilkins toppled to the dirt.

Liam covered the other men. All over the boardwalk people scattered and jumped for cover. The sheriff suddenly stood by Liam's side, gun pointed at the men on horseback. He drawled casually, "You gentlemen have something to say on this?"

All three were silent. Then, Jackson looked quickly to the others and spoke: "Nothing to say, Sheriff. We're just thirty a month cowhands. If'n you don't mind, we'll just be ridin' on."

⚛ ⚛ ⚛ ⚛ ⚛

A while later, cleaned up and sitting at dinner, Stacey looked at the three of them. Smith quickly plowed into his food. Pacheco glanced around. Liam seemed tense, she thought. He insisted on facing the door.

"Liam?" Stacey placed her hand gently on his arm. "You're thinking about something. Beecher?"

"Yep. It's not over. My gut tells me he'll show up soon."

"It is true, señor. That man cannot stomach losing. He has lost face."

Stacey nodded, then slid her hand over Liam's.

"I can't thank you enough for what you've done for me. Rally said you would come, Liam. You did and saved the ranch."

Liam looked at her for a moment before responding.

"You sure you want to keep the ranch, Stacey? You've got enough money to make a fresh start anywhere you want. The ranch would bring a fair price."

"It was Rally's dream and it became mine. There's still no better view to be had and there's still cattle in the hills that Beecher missed. I can go a few years without a drive. I think I can make a go of it." She looked at Smith. "Of course, I'll need a few good cowhands. You looking for work, Mr. Smith?"

"Yes, I am!"

෴ ෴ ෴ ෴ ෴

The next morning, Liam and Stacey were in the mercantile picking out a few items. They came out of the store to find Beecher standing, gun in hand. Liam held a stack of packages in his hands.

"Those were my cattle! You stole them!"

Liam spoke firmly, his anger rising. "Beecher! We sold

those cattle fair and square. Back off!"

Beecher seethed! How dare someone try this on him! And yet, he felt the cold breath of doom. It was as if he had a glimpse into his future – but there was no future there. His mind screamed at him to turn around, but another part of him screamed "I will not lose!"

He planted his feet firmly.

"Stacey," Liam spoke firmly. "Step to the side."

She did so.

"Liam Henry, the great gunfighter. Caught unawares with an armful of women's things." He sneered. "Well, I've got the drop on you and you can't beat a drawn gun. I'm gonna kill you!"

Liam saw the arm tense and threw the packages at Beecher and reached for his gun. Beecher's first shot went wild. His second shot crossed with Liam's. Liam Henry jerked as lead took him in the hip. Beecher stared, a look of triumph on his face. At the same time, he noticed red on his own shirtfront.

"What the…" Then he looked up as Liam fell. "I've killed the great Liam Henry!"

Liam triggered his gun again and another stain burst on Beecher's shirt.

A look of wonder briefly flickered across the big man's face before he fell, lifeless, to the ground.

◦✿◦ ◦✿◦ ◦✿◦ ◦✿◦ ◦✿◦

Curtains fluttered in the breeze. Sunlight danced around the room. All was peaceful.

Liam Henry looked around and noticed the quilt covering him. Next to the bed was a chair. It was occupied.

Stacey looked at him.

"Well, it was nip and tuck for a few days, what with the fever and all, but Doc says you'll make it."

"Where am I?"

"Boarding house in Graysville. Doc says a few more days and you'll be able to handle a wagon ride if we put in enough quilts."

"Wagon ride to where?"

"R-C ranch. Pacheco and Smith rode out a week ago to hire hands and start getting the place put back in shape."

"I can't stay, Stacey."

She was quiet for a moment, struggling with her emotions.

"I know, Liam. But you'll need some time to heal. You'll stay till you're ready to ride. And you've always got a home waiting when the trail leads this way."

JOSIE

Riding along the hillside, Josie marveled at the dazzling beauty of nature. As far as she could see, the slopes were speckled with patches of spring flowers in colors that cast unrivaled beauty across the land. This was against the eye-catching backdrop as the mountains overlapped into the distance with a changing purple hue that never ceased to amaze her. Still vigilant and aware, she stopped at a bend to cast her eyes across the valley before her.

Josie preferred the solitude of nature. It was a time of peace and she enjoyed the way her thoughts could wander and fly free. Josie Henry was a rare breed. A loner by nature, she was forced even further into solitude by her reputation. After her parents were killed by renegades from Quantrill's raiders, Josie seethed with anger. Trained by her father to shoot, she found one of the men in a saloon the next day and walked in. Men turned and laughed at this sixteen-year-old girl carrying a pistol. They stopped laughing when she pointed the gun and cocked the hammer. Announcing that the man had helped kill her pa and ma, she pulled the trigger.

Nobody knew what to do with this young lady and she stayed with the local madam until the inquest. She was allowed to go free after evidence was given that the man was, indeed, one of Quantrill's men. A week later she found another of the men, shot him in the livery and disappeared before anybody could get there. Over the past six years she had found three more men. By then her reputation had gotten out and seemed to precede her.

Few would say that she was beautiful. But none would say she was homely. She sort of rode the middle trail, turning some eyes but not others. She was not the fastest with a gun, but she could shoot straight. What played in her favor was the hesitation of men not wanting to shoot a woman. It didn't bother her in the least to take advantage of that.

Suddenly a sound came through the trees. She tensed and her horse's ears perked up. Josie turned her head and listened, waiting.

There it was again.

A cry!

Reining her horse off the trail and up the slope, she approached the top. Dismounting short of the crest, she dropped the reins to slip in a crouched walk to a clump of brush. Her right hand dropped to loose the thong of her .31 Colt.

Scanning the hillside below, Josie spotted a young boy, not fifty yards away, standing and crying. He looked to be no more than eight years old. At his feet lay a body. Two horses lay dead to one side.

Two horses, one boy and one body.

Snapping her fingers lightly, her horse came to her and she stepped out from the brush and deliberately kicked a stone.

The boy looked to her and then to the side..

Josie followed his gaze to the rifle leaning against a tree.

She smiled and said softly, "It's ok. I mean no harm."

Josie led her horse over. Once glance told her the man was dead. She then knelt in front of the boy.

"What's your name, young man?"

"Clive Baxter."

"My name is Josie Henry. Can you tell me what happened, Clive?"

"They shot my pa." Tears ran again.

Josie reached to her pocket and took out a bandanna. Wiping Clive's face and brushing his hair back, she spoke softly.

"Who shot him?"

"It was two men. They took our money. Pa saw them coming a long ways off and told me to run. They looked for me but I didn't move and they finally left."

Josie knew this type of men. Obviously not wanting witnesses, they figured to leave the boy stranded to die.

"Where's your ma?"

"She died last year. It was just me and Pa."

"I'm here now, Clive. I'll take care of you."

The terrain was rugged and rocky, so they pulled Clive's father under a rocky ledge and collapsed the overhang. Josie took the small packs and saddlebags from the horses and moved them to a campsite nearby. Caching the saddles in the brush to one side, she allowed Clive to stay at the graveside and grieve. Just before darkness set in, she rustled dinner and quietly walked to his side and put her hand on his shoulder. She led him gently to the campsite, where he sat to one side of the fire, eating little and staring into the flames. An occasional tear coursed his cheek.

Looking for sign earlier, Josie found the tracks of two horses, one that toed in. She would recognize it if she saw it again.

"Clive?"

He looked up.

"What can you tell me about these two men?"

"We saw them back in Dry Fork. Pa was buying supplies and they were in the store. When Pa pulled out his wallet to pay, I saw one of the men nudge his friend and they both watched. We were down the trail yesterday and saw them coming up the valley behind us. That's when Pa told me to run into the bushes. I heard them ask to join us. Pa didn't have a pistol, and the rifle was in the scabbard. Pa said how we'd prefer to be alone, so the one just up and shot him. I saw him take Pa's wallet. I seen them shoot the horses."

He sobbed and Josie held out her arms and he snuggled in, heaving with grief. Josie gave him some time before she spoke again.

"Would you know them if you saw them again?"

"Yes. One of them had a strange eyelid, like he'd caught it on something. He was the one who shot Pa. Miss Josie? I'd know Pa's wallet anywhere. It was special. Ma had it made for him. Real fine deer hide, and there's a star stamped on one side. Pa said it was one of a kind and he'd keep it forever."

"Where were you headed?"

"Some town called Green Valley. Uncle Lowell - that's Ma's brother - was to meet us."

"No pack horse?"

"No. Pa said best keep what we got and travel light. He just wanted to get to Uncle Lowell's."

"Do you know how much your pa was carrying in his wallet?"

"I don't know. It was all from selling the farm."

"Where are you from?"

"Back in Missouri. Ma died and crops failed. Ma's brother wrote him and said he had a ranch and could we help him. That's where we were headed. Pa had a letter."

"I put a letter in your saddlebag that was in your pa's pocket. And there was a locket – I expect it was your ma's."

Clive bent to the saddlebag and paused as he drew out the locket and the letter. Tears came again.

"Ma's locket. She wore it all the time. It has some of her hair and some of his." He fingered the chain. "And this is the letter." He handed a folded paper to Josie.

Opening it, she read the short message aloud: "Wilt, I got me a ranch. If'n you can, come to Green Valley. We talked of it. Best come before winter. Lowell Platt." She looked at Clive. "You ever met this Lowell Platt?"

"Yes. He came a year ago to visit. He and Aunt Rilda have three boys and a girl. They were fun."

"Your pa tell you where this Green Valley is?"

"Not exactly, but he said it weren't but a few more days away." He paused. "Ma'am?"

"Yes?"

"Will those men be punished for killing my pa?"

ᐤᕀᐤ ᐤᕀᐤ ᐤᕀᐤ ᐤᕀᐤ ᐤᕀᐤ

The next morning they rode toward town. The tracks of the killers were clear. Josie was wary. There were places along the trail where someone bent on mischief could hide. Her gut feeling told her these men felt assured of no pursuit and would seek to enjoy their ill-gotten gain in town.

That afternoon, they came to Dry Fork and several eyes turned as she rode in with Clive behind her.

Josie looked around. Down the street, she saw a man look her direction, then hurry towards a saloon.

Riding to the small sheriff's office, a man arose from a chair by the door and walked to meet them. His eyes took in Clive's tired and tear-stained face and the extra saddlebags. He nodded and tipped his hat.

"Morning, ma'am."

"Sheriff. My name's Josie. This is Clive Baxter. I found him yesterday on the trail. His pa was killed and the two men that did it took their money. They shot the horses and left him to die. They are either here or further down the trail. I suspect they are here."

"Been a couple no accounts ride in. They take turns sitting outside the saloon. I been wondering about them but they've caused no problems. Might be I need to talk to them. Best I talk to the young'un first. Think he's up to it?"

Josie looked to Clive with the question in her eyes.

Clive nodded. "If you can come, too?"

Josie looked at the sheriff.

He noted the cut of her trail clothes was both feminine and practical. But there was no mistaking the Colt on her hip. It sat comfortably and her hand stayed close to the walnut grip.

He nodded and motioned them to the door.

"Then come on in. I got some sassafras tea, Clive."

A few minutes later, Clive took a drink and smiled.

"Young fella, what can you tell me about these men?"

He related the experience from the start to when Josie appeared.

"One of them men at the saloon does have a strange eye. I saw him ride out of town a while back. But I suspect he'll be back. Didn't take his saddlebags."

"It's your town, Sheriff. What're your thoughts?"

"Well, I'd say the first thing is to get this boy a place to rest and get some grub in him."

"Is there a decent place to stay?"

"Miss Ethel has a small rooming house yonder. Just past the mercantile." He nodded up the street where a gray haired lady was sweeping the boardwalk. "Swing back by when you get him settled."

Josie nodded and walked her horse towards the elderly woman leaning on her broom. She smiled when she saw Clive.

"Hello, young fella."

Then she looked to Josie. Her smile was genuine. Josie smiled back.

"Miss Ethel?"

"That's me. You needing a place to stay?"

"Yes. This is Clive Baxter, and I'm Josie Henry. Clive's pa was shot up on the mountain."

Ethel's scowled.

"I am so sorry, son. You two come in, have a glass of cold water. And I might just happen to have some fresh muffins."

While Clive sat and ate a muffin, Ethel looked to Josie. She motioned with her head and led Josie into the other room.

"You know something, Ethel. What is it?"

"Two men left here yesterday and rode in again last night. Been in the saloon ever since." She smiled. "I keep my eyes open and see things. Like how them two was serious when they headed out and laughing when they came back."

Clive was tired. Josie got him settled into a room, where he lay down into the soft straw tick and his eyes began to flutter. Josie softly brushed his hair back with her fingers.

"It's alright to sleep, Clive. Miss Ethel or I will be just outside the door."

Nodding, Clive closed his eyes.

Stepping into the other room, she spoke to Ethel.

"I need to talk to the sheriff. Can you stay close in case he wakes up?"

"Certainly. Poor child."

Josie hitched her gun belt and headed down the street, aware of several sets of eyes: The curious eyes of a store clerk at the mercantile; the measuring eyes of a settler in a buckboard; the watchful eyes of the man in front of the saloon.

Was he one of the two who killed Clive's pa? Squinting from the shadow of her hat brim, she noted no strange eye. Could be the other, though. He was watching her with purpose.

She found the sheriff talking to two men.

"Ma'am? These two men said they'd head back up the trail and pick up those saddles and bridles. How far was it?" He looked down and kicked the dirt. "Boy might need the money they'll bring."

"Thank you. It's about three hours ride. You'll find the horses first. Saddles and bridles in a clump of brush off to the south. I'm beholden. I can pay."

"Not at all, ma'am. Glad to help."

After the men left to get horses, the sheriff motioned Josie to come inside.

"Fella with the bad eye came back. Expect I might wait a bit, let he and his partner settle, get a couple drinks in and put their minds on a card game."

Rolling his tobacco to one side, the sheriff aimed at the spittoon, hitting it dead center. He chuckled. "Plans made always seem to change in this business. I need to get someone to back my play, though."

He headed over to the gun cabinet.

"Sheriff, my name is Josie Henry."

Stopping in mid step, the Sheriff turned, eyes wide.

"Well, of all that's holy… I guess I should ask if you have a plan?"

"I do, Sheriff. If you're willing to follow my lead."

❧ ❧ ❧ ❧ ❧

Reaching the saloon, the man outside openly gaped at her. He did not expect it when she turned suddenly and stepped into the saloon and to the side. Letting her eyes adjust to the dim light, in the same instant she loosed the thong from her pistol. She scanned the room and placed the men and the lone saloon woman. Eyes turned to her and conversation stopped. It always caused a start for men to see her, dressed as she was and carrying the Colt, walking boldly into what was seen as a man's place.

She waited for what she knew would come next.

The man outside barged through the batwings and stood looking around. His eyes widened in surprise when he saw Josie standing just a few feet away.

"Looking for me, mister?"

"Uh, no ma'am. Just looking. Though you are mighty fine to look at." He grinned and looked across the room. His eyes lingered on a table where three men played cards.

Josie followed his gaze and a man at the table looked up. His left eyelid was twisted and torn from some past injury. The partly hidden eye underneath was sharp and clear, though. Josie heard the subtle sound of the door to the rear and knew the Sheriff would be following her lead. She addressed the men at the table.

"I came in to town with a young boy. Found him on the mountain trying to bury his pa. Said two men shot his pa and took his money. He was hiding in the brush and they shot his horses. If I hadn't come along he'd likely of died on the mountain. Obviously what they wanted." She turned to the man with the scarred eyelid, "One of the men had a bad eyelid, mister. That's you."

The man stood up, wary. As the man from outside walked over to join him, two others sat with their hands in plain sight.

"Lady, that's an accusation I don't like. You got witnesses? The boy must be mistaken."

"Your horse toes in. Plain as day on the trail."

"Lots of horses toe in."

"The boy said the men who killed his pa took his wallet. That wallet on the table next to you fits the description. I bet if you turn it over you'll find a star stamped in the leather."

"Lady, you are too big for your britches – though they do look mighty fine on you." He laughed nervously, looking around. Nobody else chuckled.

"Mister, you murdered the boy's pa."

The man's face turned ugly and he responded with firmness.

"I say you need to turn around and walk out of here and stop making accusations. A man might take offense. If'n you was a man, you'd be dead right now."

Josie stepped clear of a table, facing her accused. Her intent was clear. Stunned, men at side tables scooted their chairs and slipped out the door or to the side of the room.

"Now look here, lady. I ain't going to draw on no woman. You just take your complaint to the sheriff."

A voice spoke with firmness from the shadows off the end of the bar: "She did take it to me, and now I'm here. Got two barrels of double-ought facing your way. Best you men drop those gun belts." The sheriff slipped to the side and covered the room.

The other two men at the table realized the situation.

"Gaston, we ain't no part of this."

"Cowards both of you! Sheriff, you letting this lady run your show?"

The sound of the shotgun hammers cocking was loud and clear.

"This is my town. You think she's running the show, you just try something and see whose lead knocks you down." He then spoke harshly: "Now, you gonna drop them guns or pull them? Your choice. Save the town some money if you reach. Then we just got to push some dirt over you."

The man with the bad eye started to sweat. Staring at a murder charge, he didn't have much to lose. But no man bucked a double-barreled shotgun. He looked at Josie.

Josie saw his look and knew he was a mouse hair away from pulling iron.

"Name is Josie. Josie Henry."

Silence filled the room. Josie Henry's quest was legendary.

Gun belts thudded to the floor.

Another man sat off to one side in a corner, facing the room. With a stubble of beard, his look was seasoned. One hand held a glass, the other was below the edge of the table. He spoke, addressing the room with half an eye on the man with the scarred lid.

"Ma'am, this boy happen to be Clive Baxter?"

"He is."

"Wilt Baxter was my brother-in-law, ma'am. I came here to meet him. Name's Lowell Platt." He looked directly at the man with the scarred lid, his eyes like steel. "Wilt never did nobody no harm. Just trying to make a new start for his boy. I reckon I'm backing this play."

Josie spoke while looking at the men.

"Clive had a letter you sent to his pa."

The sheriff spoke.

"You men move away from the table. Line up by the door. This scattergun will stay at the ready."

Moving towards the door, the men were careful. Josie watched. As the sheriff rounded the end of the bar, there was a brief moment when his aim was blocked. Josie sensed it and knew. She saw the quick lurch to the side as Gaston jumped and reached for a hide out gun at his back. Her bullet took off his thumb and he screamed and grabbed his hand. Nobody else moved a muscle, knowing the effect of lead and shotgun shells in a room filled with men.

ෙ෮ ෙ෮ ෙ෮ ෙ෮ ෙ෮

The next day, Clive sat a horse outside the rooming house and Josie stood next to him. Lowell Platt held the reins of a packhorse.

Josie nodded to Lowell, then touched Clive's arm.

"Clive. I know it's going to be tough, but your pa would want you to finish the journey. Your uncle will take good care of you."

A tear showed in Clive's eye.

Josie smiled and handed him his pa's wallet. "It's a treasure, Clive. And the men who killed your pa are in jail. They wouldn't be there if it weren't for your help."

"Thank you, Miss Josie. Will I ever see you again?"

"Never know, Clive. Friends have a way of showing

up at just the right time. So I'll just say, 'till we meet again.'"

"Till we meet again, Miss Josie."

Josie clasped his hand and gave it a squeeze.

With that, Lowell Platt urged his horse on and Clive followed the packhorse. Josie watched till they reached the edge of town where the trail turned beyond the livery stable. Before the turn, Clive glanced back one more time, smiled and lifted a hand in farewell.

ALL FOR LOVE

A rock splinter ripped a furrow in her scalp just below the hairline. Only for a moment did she duck behind the large boulder before rising again to fire. To not look would allow them time to get closer. It was something she could not risk.

Sighting on a patch of brown between two trees, Carrie Stone squeezed off her shot. There was a scream followed by a long cry. That was three. Still, she did not celebrate.

There were too many.

Her husband lay wounded at her feet. A couple hours earlier, she and Leet were walking the hillside meadow, laughing and sharing words of love.

Leet came into her life four years ago and captured her heart. Initially, it was just a realization that they needed to be together and an instinctive awareness that love would grow. Deep love had blossomed and happiness filled her heart. And his, also. Though not attractive to many, Carrie saw beneath to the man inside. Yes, they both loved each other. After four years it was a strong love.

It was love that got him shot.

Leet was looking into her eyes, smiling, when a rifle cracked in the distance. He jerked and crumpled to the ground. Blood covered his head.

Their horses stood nearby. Carrie thought quickly and leapt for their rifles, a canteen and a set of saddlebags. She ducked back into the circle of rocks as several bullets whizzed by. Leet's horse startled briefly and moved off a few yards. Trained to stay ground tied and accustomed to gunfire, it would not move far. Carrie's horse stood wide-eyed in shock at first and bolted soon after she had the rifle. The packhorse ran willingly along.

Taking a few moments to explore Leet's wound, she saw that an inch further and he'd have been dead. He still might be. It was a nasty wound.

It was now up to her to defend him.

Glancing up and jacking a shell into the rifle, Carrie waited. She saw movement down the hillside. Grasping the saddlebags, she opened them and found the box of shells Leet always carried, thankful again for her man's precautions. Attracting stares and confrontation because of his size and the hair that covered his body, Leet knew the value of being prepared for both the expected and the unexpected.

There were a handful of men below, spreading out and taking positions.

Who were they and why were they after Leet? Or were they after her?

These four years had been a blessing, as Leet took on the role of banker in the small town and dedicated himself to doing well and changing the lives of the townsfolk. He was beloved.

Who was attacking them?

For many months, she sensed discontent in Leet. One evening on the porch, Carrie and he spoke of a place in the distant mountains to raise their children. Thinking she was unable to have children, they discovered otherwise. Their son Cale, born these two years back, was a delight and they planned to add another to their lives. In fact, a child was growing inside her and they were determined to view this mountain country while she was still able. The hope was to move into their own cabin a few months after the birth. So they ventured out on this journey of exploration together. They'd left Cale behind with close friends.

Bullets cracked against the rocks. Carrie knew such a fusillade was meant to keep her crouching so the men could work closer. She could not let it happen. Moving to the right, she peered through a small gap and slowly took aim. A near miss, it did not take the man out of action but would serve as a warning and cause him to hesitate. Moving again, she evaded the return shots and fired again. Another burst from below sent fragments all directions.

Rocks were great for stopping bullets, but often the ricochet's caused more damage. Carrie was lucky so far, receiving only the grazing wound to her brow.

Move and fire, move and fire. Carrie kept the pattern varied, knowing predictability was fatal. As the only daughter among boys, she was thankful for her competitive spirit and the practical father who encouraged her. Though not the best shot, she held her own with her brothers in filling the dinner table.

Wiping blood from her eyes, she ripped a strip from her skirt and wrapped it around her brow. Mingled blood and sweat smeared her face. The men below were spreading to the right, threatening her flank. A little further and one of the attackers would be able to fire behind the rocks.

Carrie looked down at Leet, fearful. He needed care, and she could not give it while defending them. A strong woman, a tear welled in her eye.

There was nothing she could do and it was just a matter of time. She whispered a silent prayer.

"Drop it, lady!" A man stood to her left, his gun pointed. She heard another step to her right.

"You can't get us both."

Carrie dropped her rifle.

⚜ ⚜ ⚜ ⚜ ⚜

Two more men rode up leading an empty horse. One wore a bloody bandage. The leader was a tall evil looking man.

"Well, lady. You played hob with us, killed a good man. But it all comes down to we've got you now." He motioned to a young man barely out of his teens. "Peterson! Get her on Clint's horse! We move out now."

Carrie looked up at the man and met his eye.

"What do you want with us?"

"We want nothing to do with that…Grizzly. It's you we want."

"Rafe, we been going all day. Ain't we got time for coffee?" The speaker was a slender man with a neck crooked to one side.

Rafe looked hard at the man, who met his eyes only briefly before averting.

"Blake, you want to do as I say or stay here and die

with this fella?"

"Sorry, Rafe, I wasn't thinkin' rightly."

Carrie looked down at Leet, blood all over his head and unconscious. "What about my husband."

Rafe smiled. "He's a dead man. Solid head shot. He can die alone or maybe the coyotes will help it along."

"You can't just leave my husband wounded out here!"

Rafe pulled his pistol and aimed it at Leet. "Want me to help him enter the Pearly Gates? Or do you want him to have some time to think of his beloved. Won't be much time guessin' by the blood, but I do have a tiny bit of sympathy." He was smirking.

"Leave him, please. He's dying anyway." Her heart was broken. She knelt by Leet's side and leaned to kiss his cheek. His eye flickered. Her knee pushed to his side as she arose.

They tied her hands to the saddle and off they rode.

༖ ༖ ༖ ༖ ༖

The moonlight cast an eerie light upon the land as Leet's eyes flickered again. Where was he? Where was Carrie? He remembered holding her, then the sharp pain. All was darkness after that, except a brief view of a man's face and Carrie leaning over him. That and the bump of her knee at his side.

He lay for many minutes trying to clear the fog from his mind. He had to think!

It was a cold night. He knew he was hit hard and his head pounded. It was likely the cold that saved him. Slowly reaching to his head, he winced.

Where was Carrie? Whoever shot him must have her. Either that or… Struggling to raise his head, he glanced where he could. No sign of her.

The fog filled his mind again.

Coyotes howled in the distance. He awoke sharply. Coyotes! They would smell him out. What the bullet didn't complete, they would. Despite his wound, he must move or die.

And find Carrie.

Working his elbows beneath him, his hand brushed something in the grass. Carrie's derringer! She must have dropped it. He remembered the knee pushing him. She must have done that to tuck the derringer under his side. So she was alive. And he had two shots.

It took some minutes to get to a sitting position and look around. The coyotes were closer. Finding a broken branch between the rocks, Leet drew it to him to use as a weapon and a crutch. Grasping the rock nearest him, he wavered at the edge of consciousness as he rose to his feet and lay leaning on the rock. Dizziness overwhelmed him.

ֆֆ ֆֆ ֆֆ ֆֆ ֆֆ

"What do you want with me?" Carrie sat against a small tree. She was worried about Leet, but knew she needed to survive.

"Well, lady, you got something we want."

"What could you want from me? I don't know any of you."

"A few years ago, you had a man visit you at your ranch. It was before you married your…" He looked back down the trail as coyotes howled, and smiled, "former husband. Man rode a gray mule. Stayed just overnight. You remember?"

Carrie thought a moment. "We had a lot of people stay now and then. Fed a lot of wandering cowboys."

"Had a shock of bushy hair, one side all white."

Carrie remembered the man by his strange hair. The man had stopped and stayed in their barn overnight. Friendly enough, but odd enough that they slept with the door locked. Her remembrance showed in her eyes.

Rafe smiled. "You recollect it."

"I do remember. A strange man."

Rafe nodded. "He was odd, but he was also rich. And he told us – with a bit of persuasion – that he'd told you the location of his cache of gold."

Carrie asked, "Didn't he tell you?"

"Started to, but we got sort of overambitious with the knife – Dirk cut a bit too much – and the old codger pegged out before we got the last step. Got so mad I had to shoot Dirk just to get over it."

Carrie shivered. "I don't recall what he said."

"Well, lady. That may be rightly so. But I think we might just have to refresh your memory." He grinned. "We'll start tomorrow. Ride that way and let your memory work. In the meantime, it'll do you no good to try and get away. Too much empty country around." Smirking, he looked her square in the eyes. "Lots of varmints looking for a meal out there." Pointing to Peterson, he ordered, "You take first watch. If the lady so much as squirms, belt her across the head."

Carrie lay back against the tree and closed her eyes. She recalled the man staying over, and knew they had a conversation. He talked softly to her by the well, but she wasn't really paying attention. In fact, she thought he was crazy and was just rambling. She recalled something about a fish out of water and a jagged pillar of quartz. The rest she just dismissed as meaningless.

Leet! Where was he? Was he still alive? When she'd bent to kiss him and saw his eye flicker, she let her derringer slip out and quickly pushed it under his side with her knee. She must not lose hope! If Leet was able, he would come. She must trust in his skills and strength. He wouldn't die easy.

❧ ❧ ❧ ❧ ❧

Leet did not get far that night. He followed the path of the horses until he collapsed in the dark and lay until the sun beat upon him. The nighttime chill left the land but he was cold to the bone.

He must find water.

Stumbling to his feet, his eyes slowly cleared and he glimpsed a clump of trees in what appeared to be an old streambed. Probably a mile away, it took him all morning to reach it. When he reached the shade, he sank to his knees and fell to his face where a small seep escaped an underground stream. There was barely enough for a couple drinks in a small hollow. He drank and began to move the dirt with his hands to build a bigger hollow. Then he slept.

A sound came to him in his sleep and he fought to wakefulness as the sound increased. He looked over.

Their packhorse!

Speaking softly, he slowly got to his knees and the horse, finding the water-filled hollow, lowered its head to drink. Leet carefully approached the horse and, though it shied slightly, it had been with them long enough that his voice was familiar. Grasping the reins, he let the horse drink its fill as he sat against a tree.

Leet's head began to spin and he tied the reins to his leg and slept once more. He did not stir until the insects began to speak their evening messages to the land.

He desperately wanted to rest more, but his heart held sway.

He must go on. Carrie would be depending on him. She knew he would come.

Leet reached for the reins.

⚛ ⚛ ⚛ ⚛ ⚛

For a day they rode. Carrie's heart anguished, knowing Leet would be far behind, if at all. He was a man alone and with a long trail to find her. She glimpsed back down the trail. Rafe, glancing over, chuckled. "Lady, that man of yours took a bad one. He's got no horse, no gun. Best not keep your hopes up. In fact, you ought to think real hard about what that old fella told you."

Carrie thought about more than that. She knew they had no intention of letting her live. Once they found the gold they would kill her and move on.

She must give time for Leet to catch up.

"I need rest. My head is throbbing. If you want me to remember, I need to sleep. You killed my husband, grabbed me and somehow you want me to sit back and suddenly remember? I need time!"

"She's wiped out, Rafe. She needs to rest." It was Peterson.

Turning in his saddle, Rafe's piercing eyes spit venom at the young man. He pointed his pistol at Peterson's head and pulled the hammer back.

"Peterson…you're the new man on the block, so I'll not kill you this time. But if you ever so much as question me again or butt in where you ain't asked, I will kill you like a dog. You'll never see your nineteenth birthday. Now… back off!"

Peterson pulled away, eyes wide with fear.

Rafe looked at Carrie. "We'll let you rest. It better help you remember."

"It'll help."

"We'll rest one day. Use it wisely." He called to another man, who looked up. "Dobbs! We'll rest a day here. See if you can rustle up some fresh meat. Take Blake with you."

"Will do, Rafe."

Carrie laid back and pretended to sleep. She thought of Peterson. He wasn't the same as the others. It was something to remember.

๛ ๛ ๛ ๛ ๛

If not for his natural strength, he would have collapsed long ago and lay until his bones bleached in the sun. But Leet Stone was not the average man. Never one to take the easy way, he faced this trial with the same determination with which he faced life. Many years on the back of a horse and struggling to survive had given him an internal strength. Being forced to fight taught him to not give up and to take the bull by the horns.

Hours blended one into another. Leet cut across the countryside until he found a trail and, setting his jaw, followed.

oⱡo oⱡo oⱡo oⱡo oⱡo

"What are you doing?" Rafe was angry.

Carrie had awakened in the night, edged over and placed a large chunk on the fire, sending sparks and flames high into the night and illuminating the darkness.

"I'm cold. Besides, I remember the man told me something as he looked into the flames. I'm trying to remember."

"Remember, or signal?"

Looking firmly into the man's eyes, Carrie spoke with malevolence. "Signal who? Just who do you think would possibly be here to signal? Don't you remember what you did? My husband is dead."

Rafe chuckled. "I guess you're right. How's your other memories coming?"

"He said something about a fish out of water. But I have no clue what that means."

"What else?"

"Something about a jagged rock of quartz."

"Water. Something to do with water and a quartz out-cropping. What else?"

"I'm trying to remember. Seems he said something else, but it's not coming to me yet."

"Tomorrow it will. Guarantee it."

Carrie stared into the flames. Was the fire big enough for Leet to see? Was he even out there? She stared into the flames, praying and thinking. Drifting back in time, she remembered that night long ago, before Leet came along; before her first husband died. That odd man rode in one evening. Just a drifter in their eyes, but they never sent anyone away hungry. He sat over coffee and told a story. Snippets of the conversation came to her, slowly piecing together and then, suddenly, her eyes flew open. She remembered! She knew where the gold was! Breathing steadily, she calmed herself, vowing to never reveal the location to this evil man.

৹⊹৹ ৹⊹৹ ৹⊹৹ ৹⊹৹ ৹⊹৹

Leet finally slept. It was fitful sleep, his heart battling with his body. Always, Carrie lingered in the edge of his mind.

Awakening in the dark of night, he mounted and glanced around.

He whispered into the night: "Carrie, where are you?"

As if in response, in the distance he saw a burst of flame.

He urged the horse forward, one hand reaching into his pocket to touch the derringer.

ᐶᐧᐶ ᐶᐧᐶ ᐶᐧᐶ ᐶᐧᐶ ᐶᐧᐶ

"It's time to remember, lady." Rafe threw sticks on the fire.

A sliver of sun paused on the horizon as if trying to decide whether it was time to bring on the day. The wild land relinquished slumber with hesitance.

There were groans as Rafe kicked boots and urged the men into activity. Silent, they stared into the new flames as Dobbs set the coffee on.

"Blake, get that little blade of yours all polished up." When the man looked at him, Rafe spit. "Don't fret. I'll do the cutting. Don't want it messed up this time."

The others looked to Rafe, then to Carrie. Peterson's eyes lingered longer. Accustomed to the lack of scruples of the outlaw trail, there were still lines of right and wrong. But their fear of Rafe, mingled with the hope of gold, tied their tongues.

A cricket sounded softly in the silence. Just a single, short and hardly perceptible chirp.

Carrie heard the cricket. Her heart leapt, but she was careful not to show any reaction.

Leet! He often had used that sound when he would come in from the dark as a little warning to her that the steps were his. So he was here!

ᐶᐧᐶ ᐶᐧᐶ ᐶᐧᐶ ᐶᐧᐶ ᐶᐧᐶ

Rafe spoke again as he reached for the coffee. "Peterson! I know you can't handle this. You go watch the horses." Peterson walked by Carrie and faded into the brush. As he passed, he dropped something.

A knife! She shifted slightly and covered it with the fold of her dress.

"Boss?" It was Blake. "Think I'll fetch water from the creek yonder."

"Do that! And bring the bucket back. We'll need to wash soon."

Sneering, Rafe turned to Dobbs. "What about you?"

"Reckon I'll stay. Never seen a woman cut before."

Rafe checked the blade. Sharp!

Walking over to Carrie, he grinned and flashed the knife before her. "Does this spark your memory?"

Carrie stared at Rafe with a panicked glare. "I need a few more minutes! Please! Oh, please don't cut me."

A thud sounded towards the creek. This time Rafe looked up.

"Clumsy!"

꧁ ꧁ ꧁ ꧁ ꧁

The young man with the horses was easy. His mind was back at the fire and filled with doubts. Leet slammed a fist to his head and he fell like a sack.

Spotting a man headed to the creek, he came up behind and raised a large branch. Blake, sensing something, turned and caught the deadly blow across the bridge of his nose.

Leet breathed heavily and moved to the left.

❧ ❧ ❧ ❧ ❧

Rafe waited impatiently. Sparse minutes later, he suddenly looked around. Walking towards the brush where the horses were tied, he hollered. Receiving no response, he hissed to Dobbs, "Go check on him!"

Dobbs stood, staring the other way.

Rafe turned.

"I said…" The words were never completed.

At the edge of camp stood Leet, his face a mask of dried blood and dirt. But it was the look that froze Rafe.

A Grizzly bear. Walking towards him. Stunned by the apparition, he finally reached for his gun.

The derringer fired. Rafe crumpled lifelessly to the ground.

Dobbs fumbled with his gun. Carrie whipped the blade of Peterson's knife across his arm. He screamed and pointed his gun at Carrie. Leet half turned and fired the other barrel. Dobbs fell, dead.

❧ ❧ ❧ ❧ ❧

"Carrie are you ok? Did they hurt you? Is the baby ok?"

He held her close.

"Oh, Leet! When I heard that cricket my heart pounded. They were going to cut on me. But you got here before they could hurt me. The baby is fine."

"It's ok now." He hugged her close.

"Leet? The young man…is he…dead?"

"I don't think so. Just out cold."

"He tried to protect me. He dropped the knife for me."

᚛ᚑ ᚛ᚑ ᚛ᚑ ᚛ᚑ ᚛ᚑ

Later, Carrie knelt by Leet's side, bathing and bandaging his head wound. They had sent Peterson down the trail, alive and seeing the error of his ways. They gave him the extra horses, urging him to make a fresh start with the money he received from their sale.

Leet sat quietly, relishing in the gift of this woman who had come close to being torn from his life.

"Carrie, I love you."

"Oh, Leet. I love you, too."

She wiped his lips and they kissed gently.

Sitting back a moment, she rinsed the rag and told him what the men had wanted.

"How could they expect you to remember?"

"Strangely enough, Leet…I do remember. I remember where the man told me the gold was hidden. He told me – I think – knowing his trail was coming to an end. We need to take a short side trip – a treasure hunt. Isn't it amazing how God takes a horrible situation and wrings a blessing out of it?"

᚛ᚑ ᚛ᚑ ᚛ᚑ ᚛ᚑ ᚛ᚑ

Three days later, Leet and Carrie saddled the horses.

Rested and fed, Leet looked over at Carrie and reached across for her hand. Holding it briefly, he looked at her tenderly.

"That was your favorite skirt you tore up for bandages."

She smiled and cried. Happy tears flowed.

Reining up slowly, she grasped Leet's hand and placed it upon her slightly swelling abdomen.

"That skirt would have been too small before long anyhow."

June Bug and the Railroad Man

The ten-year-old girl fast-footed it around the corner of the barn, then turned up the hill into the trees. Looking back, she saw she wasn't followed. The Quigley's had fallen on hard times, and she'd quietly left a pie on the sill. A smile crossed her face.

Her given name was Betsy June Larrimore, but early on she became known as "June Bug." June Bug always showed a tendency to kindness. She was always looking for ways to do something nice. Perpetually excited for each new day, her smile was winsome, and everybody loved her. Her mother, Sally, worked for Marge in the diner in New Haven and her father, Walt, was the town sheriff and sometimes deputy U.S. Marshall.

June Bug's giving nature was a wonder to others, seemingly wrought from sorrow. The loss of her little sister, Marietta, to diphtheria when June Bug was only five years old seemed to have left an indelible appreciation of the shortness of time on this delightful child.

June Bug popped into the diner and immediately was hailed by a half-dozen customers. Looking around, she smiled as she made a beeline to her favorite table. June Bug was enamored of the middle-aged but robust rancher who came to town with his wife on Wednesdays for the midday meal and to catch up on the latest news. Known to most as Otis Henry, a few called him "Bull," a name earned in his youth in the Civil War. He and Ella had come into this land when it was wild and worked to build a successful ranch and a family of well-thought-of sons.

As she approached the table, Otis interrupted his conversation and slid his chair back. The girl slid expertly to his knee and gave him a big hug.

"I love you, Papa Otis." Though not family by blood, the deep abiding friendship of their families was strong.

"I love you, too, June Bug."

June Bug looked around. To the left was another favorite who went by the name of Tetch. He was a former slave who became a trusted friend and was the first ranch hand of Otis and Ella. Now gray-haired, a bad heart limited his work, but he was treated with deference by the family and accepted by the locals. Early on the color of his skin made a difference but not anymore. He lived in a small cabin on the Henry ranch but shared the table at the main house often. It was understood by all that to disrespect Tetch was to disrespect Otis and Ella.

June Bug smiled wide. "Uncle Tetch! You're looking much better today!"

"Well, girl, I am feelin' better."

Ella Henry walked in from the kitchen where she'd gone to say a few words to Marge.

"Good morning, June Bug!"

"Good morning, Grammy."

June Bug turned and smiled to Otis. He read something in her eyes.

"I bet you've already done a good deed today, little girl?"

She winked.

The door opened and Walt came in, looking concerned. His face changed and he grinned as his daughter slid off Otis' lap and ran up to him.

"Daddy!"

"Hey, Precious!"

She looked to her dad's face.

"Are you alright, Daddy?"

"I'm alright, Baby June Bug. Just a lot going on. Why don't you go check on your mom while I talk to Otis."

June Bug nodded and headed to the kitchen, seeing her mother making pie crusts. Her stomach was growing large with child and June Bug smiled at the thought of being a big sister again. Stopping just inside the door, she turned back to listen.

Walt grabbed a chair and sat, nodding to Ella and Tetch. Leaning forward on his elbows and running his fingers through his hair, his expression spoke volumes.

Otis reached over and patted his shoulder.

"You look like the dog stole your steak, Walt. What's up?"

"We got problems, Otis. I spoke with Dunkerson this morning."

Dunkerson, working for the railroad and in a sense for the big eastern cattle syndicate, had been here for a week. He spent much time on a horse, scouting the route of the tracks. It was his decision that would make the difference. Otis had shared a meal with the man.

"What'd he say?"

"Says they might best put the railroad spur a hundred miles south. Says it'd be easier to lay the track. Our location will require a lot of fill. He said it would cost a lot extra in labor."

Otis leaned back in his chair and frowned. While they had a railroad station, the spur would be run a few miles out of town for a massive stockyard. It was the key for New Haven to become the new cattle center of the region.

"Is the decision final, Walt?"

"Not yet. But I can't think of anything we can do to change his mind."

"We've already fed him the best beef, given land for the tracks and stockyards and promised him timber for the ties."

"We sure have. Everybody wants the spur. Whoever gets it will become the major town of the region, while others will fade or die out. Fella named Harvey has been building fancy hotels at major towns. Dunkerson told me this morning that there's a good chance whichever town gets the spur will get a fancy hotel right away. Other towns know what's at stake, too, and are offering the same as us. We need something special to make us stand out."

Otis Henry had fought soldiers and Indians, drought and hail. He had survived stampedes and attacks on his ranch by those intent upon killing him. He faced it all with determination and a refusal to quit. But the same tactics now were limited. And it was true that to bring the railroad spur in further south would mean easier track laying. There was logic in that decision. He said as much.

"It would take something special to win him over," said Tetch.

"I don't know what else we could do." Walt touched his fingertips together. "We need something that defies logic."

ᦉᦉ ᦉᦉ ᦉᦉ ᦉᦉ ᦉᦉ

June Bug furrowed her brow in thought. Slipping around other tables, she went to the door, pausing for a brief moment and looking back. Tetch caught her eye, then watched, curious, as she went out the door.

Listening to her parents and others, June Bug knew this railroad was a big thing. Her daddy always sat down and explained issues in language she could understand. With the high demand for beef back in the east, the place that had the railroad spur and stockyard would be where everybody came with cattle to ship. It was important, he said.

Sitting on the edge of the boardwalk, she looked across the street and saw Dunkerson, the railroad man, ride his horse out of town. Having watched the man since he arrived, she was taken aback by his perpetual look of seriousness. He never smiled. Never. Wouldn't it be great if…?

Suddenly a big grin lit her face and she strode off.

ᦉᦉ ᦉᦉ ᦉᦉ ᦉᦉ ᦉᦉ

That afternoon, hot and tired from the ride, Avery Dunkerson stiffly dismounted at the livery and passed the reins to the hostler, a man named Ike who was reported to have been there since the dawn of time. Avery said nothing. All business, he took it for granted that others would do what they were paid to do.

A man of deep responsibility, Avery Dunkerson came from a dispassionate family and fit well into his role as scout for railroad and the cattle syndicate. Towns were willing to do just about anything to get the tracks. He rarely had to buy a meal and received the best rooms. That is, until he made a decision. Then he became as a leper until he left town – which was usually fast.

During today's ride, he thought long and hard. Looking the land over once again, it was clear that the expense to put the spur in here would be much higher than further south. Well aware of the benefit of the railroad to the prosperity and future of any town, he was hardened to the plights and begging's. Bribes were commonly offered. He knew all the tricks and took pride in making all decisions based upon clear business practice. It was all business to him. His higher-ups knew this and trusted his decisions. They also compensated him well.

Still, something about this town was different. Nobody begged; nobody tried to slip him bribes; nobody tried anything. Oh, they did serve good steak, but that was expected. Readily able to spot fakes, he found none of that in New Haven. This was a town with hardened western men. Honesty and integrity were paramount. He'd met Otis Henry and read the man quickly. A patriarch of the area, his influence was wide and lent an aura of grit and determination to the entire region. All the area ranchers were solid, hard-working and ready to help a friend. In his rides, Avery had cornered simple cowhands and asked questions and had been regaled by stories of the town standing up to every danger, of having banded together in the face of trouble. He had to admit he'd also experienced the best biscuits he'd ever tasted. That Marge was incredible!

There was a different feel to this area. It was a feel of impending and budding prosperity. Still, the decision needed to be made with practical business logic. All of that pointed south.

He caught the merest glimpse of a young girl dashing down the alley as he approached the boardwalk of the small hotel. Not even nodding to the clerk, he trod slowly up the steps and, reaching his door, saw it was ajar. He stopped and hesitantly pushed the door open. Nobody was there, but on the nightstand was a big slice of apple pie and a glass of sweet milk.

He grunted and walked over. The glass was cool, the pie warm. Fresh. An attempt to influence his decision. A small crease appeared at the corner of his mouth. Bribery wouldn't work, but no need to waste a perfectly good slice of pie.

༺ ༺ ༺ ༺ ༺

Dunkerson walked into Marge's the next morning and took a seat near the window. He liked to watch the activity of the towns he was investigating. There was early activity in the street, and he once again saw nobody loitering.

Lost in his thoughts, he was somewhat startled when a little girl came to his table. He was sure she was the same he'd seen last evening in the alley. She greeted him with a wide and genuine smile.

"Good morning, Mr. Dunkerson. Coffee?"

"Yes, please, young lady."

Returning a moment later with the pot, heavy and tilted dangerously, she set it on the table and shook her wrist.

"That's a mite heavy for you. Here, let me pour."

"Thank you, sir. And you can call me June Bug."

"June Bug? That's a unique name."

"My real name is Betsy June, but everybody calls me June Bug. Would you like your usual?"

"Yes, please, June Bug. Maybe throw on an extra biscuit."

"The biscuits are the best, aren't they?"

"Yes, they truly are."

"My mom works here. She made the biscuits this morning. I like them slathered with grape jam. Have you tried that?"

"Not yet, but I think I'd like to!"

"The pie is amazing, too, Mr. Dunkerson." She glanced carefully to the kitchen door. "Mom and Marge make the best. Mom says a piece of pie from here will change your life."

He looked at her with a question in his eyes, but June Bug turned and pranced to the kitchen, humming cheerfully.

Avery Dunkerson watched her. A very happy child, he thought.

᪥᪥ ᪥᪥ ᪥᪥ ᪥᪥ ᪥᪥

Later that afternoon June Bug approached Avery Dunkerson. He was sitting on a bench under a big shade tree at the edge of town. The bench was well used.

"Hey, Mr. Dunkerson."

Avery Dunkerson looked up.

"Hey, June Bug."

"Whatcha doing?"

"Just thinking. Big decisions to make."

"This is a good spot."

"How's that?"

"Well, my daddy tells me that there is something special about this spot. All the townspeople come here when they make big decisions. I think Papa Henry started it."

"Papa Henry? Is Otis Henry your grandfather?"

"Not really…but he is. I don't have any real grandparents here. But Papa Henry is real to me. I love him. Everybody does."

"I see."

"Daddy sat on this bench when we lost my sister."

Dunkerson looked at her sharply.

"You lost a sister?"

"She got the diphtheria. I miss her. But now Mom is going to have another baby."

"So your daddy sat here after your sister died?"

"Yes. He said it was here in this spot that he decided to get out of a hole and go on. I think that means he knew he had me and mom to take care of still and he needed to say goodbye to Marietta."

Dunkerson looked at her. A marvelously perceptive child!

"That must have been hard on your dad."

"I have a wonderful daddy. Mr. Dunkerson?"

"Hm?"

"Daddy says you have to make the decision about where the railroad spur goes. I don't understand it all, but I watch. It's a big thing, isn't it?"

"It is a very big decision."

"It's hard to make decisions at times, because it can hurt people."

Dunkerson looked kindly at June Bug.

"You are a wise young lady, June Bug. It is, indeed, a difficult decision. Which is why I have to decide using very practical business ideas."

"What does that mean?"

"It means, for example, that several towns want this railroad spur. There are people in each of those towns and they all have the same thing – a willingness to give land and other items to make this work. So, I have to use more practical means to make a decision – like the land that the tracks have to cover. Each arroyo or canyon costs time and money. So sometimes it comes down to where will it cost the railroad company the least to build the tracks. It comes down to practical business."

"What about the people?"

"What do you mean, June Bug?"

"It seems to me that in some places people are different. Like here. Everybody loves and cares for each other." She patted the bench. "Do you mind if I sit, too?"

Dunkerson scooted over. "Please do." He looked down at her. "By the way, do you have any idea who left the pie and sweet milk for me last night?"

June Bug grinned. "I did."

"Did someone put you up to it?"

"Nope. In fact, after I took the pie, I heard mom yell. I guess she was saving it for after dinner." June Bug laughed heartily. "She didn't say anything to me, but when she cut the pie and passed it around, I said I didn't need a slice. Mom grinned at me." Looking up to his face, she met his eyes. "You see, Mr. Dunkerson, every time I see your face you look unhappy. And one thing I do know is that a good slice of mom's apple pie with sweet milk always makes the customers happy. Mom says biscuits in the morning, pie after dinner makes a happy man."

"Your mom is right."

"Besides, I really like to do nice things for people." She put her hand through his elbow and looked up at him. "Did it make you smile?"

"A little."

"Smiling is good for you." She suddenly looked serious. "Mr. Dunkerson? Can I ask you a question?"

"Sure."

"Do you like it here?"

"It is a nice little town."

"Is it different from other places?"

Dunkerson paused and looked down the street. When he answered, he was thoughtful. "June Bug, I think it is different. There is something stronger here than in many places. There is something about the people."

"Is it better for the railroad to have strong people? Is that practical business?"

"A strong town always lends strength to any business."

June Bug smiled and looked coy.

"Do you like the biscuits and pie at the diner?"

Dunkerson drew back with the change.

"Probably the best I've ever had." He looked serious. "That's a strange question out of the blue."

"Well, if more people could taste Mom's baking, they'd come back for more. Then Marge could build a bigger diner and more people would eat her biscuits and pie. Would that be a good thing?"

"Your mom would like that."

"And Papa Henry is always helping other people. In fact, everybody is like that around here. My daddy says it is always better to give than to receive."

"I was told that, too."

"Well, if you give this town the railroad spur, then the town can give more also. Wouldn't that be wonderful. To give more! Sometimes practical business is more about the people." June bug clapped with excitement. "I love to help Mom and Daddy. In fact, I like to help everybody! I got to go, Mr. Dunkerson. Time to go help Mom start dinner." She started to run off, then skidded to a stop. "Mr. Dunkerson?"

"Yes?"

"You eating at the diner tonight?"

"I expect so."

"I'll make sure you have a fresh glass of sweet milk with your pie. I think Mom's making blueberry."

"Thank you, June Bug."

Dunkerson watched her run off, then shifted his eyes into the distance, thinking. He sat for quite some time.

And he smiled.

ᚼᛏᛉ ᚼᛏᛉ ᚼᛏᛉ ᚼᛏᛉ ᚼᛏᛉ

At dinner time, Avery Dunkerson walked into Marge's and sat at a corner table. Other patrons nodded to him. Several spoke kindly to him. Marge brought the coffee and filled his cup.

"Excellent pot roast tonight, Mr. Dunkerson! Carrots and potatoes smothered in gravy. Want me to load a plate?"

"Yes, please. And is June Bug around?"

Marge looked at him. "She's in the kitchen. Is everything ok?"

"Oh, absolutely. I was wondering if she might be convinced to join me for a slice of pie – if there is any left. I hear it's blueberry."

Marge laughed. "Word gets around! Sally makes a mean blueberry pie. Better than mine, though I can't figure out why."

A few minutes later, June Bug came in, straining to carry the dinner plate in one hand and a biscuit plate in the other. As she approached, Avery Dunkerson grasped the plates and helped set them down.

"Are you going to join me for pie?"

June Bug smiled and winked. "I'm going to cut some of the biggest slices of pie ever! And I got the sweet milk."

Avery Dunkerson leaned closer to her and whispered: "Even if New Haven doesn't get the railroad spur?"

June bug nodded.

"Friends are most important. And you're my friend. Pie is second, though." Then she laughed. "That's just practical business!"

They both laughed.

ᘒᕲ ᘒᕲ ᘒᕲ ᘒᕲ ᘒᕲ

The next day, Avery Dunkerson came into Marge's. He looked around to find an empty table. He spotted June Bug at a table with Otis Henry. June Bug waved him over.

"Join us, Mr. Dunkerson?"

He shook hands with Otis and sat down. June Bug smiled.

"Corned beef hash today, Mr. Dunkerson." She smiled and whispered, "And I'll get you extra biscuits."

Wiping his plate later with a biscuit, Avery glanced at Otis and looked at June Bug. Then he smiled at Otis.

"Mr. Henry, this girl is extraordinary." He saw the questioning look and chuckled. "I believe there is a saying about 'out of the mouths of babes.'"

"I'm not following you, Mr. Dunkerson."

Avery Dunkerson smiled and turned to June Bug.

"June Bug? I wonder if you might do me a favor?"

"Absolutely."

"Would you please spread the word that I'd like to talk to the town elders and local ranchers. Tomorrow afternoon, if possible. And I'd like you to be there also." He smiled and looked her in the eyes. "We need to sign some papers."

June Bug's eyes widened. "You mean…?"

"Yes. And June Bug?" He smiled. "Might be nice to have some pie at the meeting."

"And sweet milk, Mr. Dunkerson?"

"Of course."

June Bug nodded. "I'll tell Mom…pie and sweet milk are just practical business."

ABOUT THE AUTHOR

Mark has always loved the old West. Spending his high school and college years in Idaho, he became enamored with the mountains and the characters of a more rugged life. With a B.A. in History from Boise State University and a Masters in Counseling Psychology from Ball State University, he has experience as counselor, seminar speaker, adjunct college  faculty, pastor, hospice chaplain and now author. An avid reader all his life, Mark has spent countless hours with his favorite author, Louis L'Amour, and seeks to share the adventure and clear morals of the classic west. He and his wife reside in Indiana

Follow him on Facebook at **Mark Herbkersman Author**.

Made in the USA
Monee, IL
15 February 2020